DIRTY WORK

JULIA BELL

DIRTY WORK

Walker & Company
New York

First published in Great Britain in 2007 by Young Picador, an imprint of Pan Macmillan Limited
Published in the U.S.A. in 2008 by Walker Publishing Company, Inc.
Distributed to the trade by Holtzbrinck Publishers

"I Live Off You" lyrics by Poly Styrene © 1977
From *Diary of the 70s* by Poly Styrene © 2005
www.x-rayspex.com

For information about permission to reproduce selections from this book, write to
Permissions, Walker & Company, 175 Fifth Avenue, New York, New York 10010

Library of Congress Cataloging-in-Publication Data
Bell, Julia.
Dirty work / Julia Bell.
p.   cm.
Summary: Two teenaged girls with little in common must find a way to work together
if they are ever to escape their captors after being abducted into an international
prostitution ring.
ISBN-13: 978-0-8027-9741-4 • ISBN-10: 0-8027-9741-5
[1. Prostitution—Fiction. 2. Kidnapping—Fiction. 3. Interpersonal relations.] I. Title.
PZ7.B38899Dir 2008   [Fic]—dc22   2007020137

Visit Walker & Company's Web site at www.walkeryoungreaders.com

Typeset by Intype Libra Ltd.
Printed in the U.S.A. by Quebecor World Fairfield
2 4 6 8 10 9 7 5 3 1

All papers used by Walker & Company are natural, recyclable products
made from wood grown in well-managed forests. The manufacturing processes
conform to the environmental regulations of the country of origin.

669452

Thanks to:

*Liviu Tipurita, Emma Hargrave, Rachel Bradford,
Jeremy Sheldon, Lucie Bennett, Monique Roffey,
Tina Jackson, and Paschal Kane*

And thanks to E. F., puss

I live off you

I live off you
And you live off me
And the whole world
Lives off of everybody

See we gotta be exploited
See we gotta be exploited
By somebody by somebody
By somebody

PROLOGUE

Oksana

"When I wake up, she is gone." That's what I tell him, over and over. It's the truth, even though I know, right now, he doesn't believe me.

He stamps around the room, kicking the furniture and shouting. Don't I know how much money he will lose? Don't I know how much she's *worth*? I shouldn't have been sleeping! I should have been watching!

And by then he's given himself enough reasons, and he punches me in the arm and then he slaps me across the face. Tomorrow we are supposed to be going to London. Zergei has made a good deal with his contacts. Ten thousand for two, delivery included. "First class," he said, laughing, to the man on the phone.

We've only been in Amsterdam for a week, just so he can sort out some paperwork, and then we get the ferry to England. When we get there, after we've been handed over, Zergei's going to help me escape, that's what he says, and we're going to run away from "all this shit" and start a new life someplace. But ten thousand isn't enough in any currency to run away with me and start a new life. The moment he gets that money in his hands, he's going to walk away and fly to Rio, where the girls hang out on the beaches in bikinis, and you can get all the tits you want for free. I'm not stupid; I can see how life works.

Which is why, if Marie had found a way to run away, I wish she'd told me, because I would have gone with her too.

He comes back later, rushing up the steep stairs to the top of the house. He's swearing and shouting my name, which is bad news.

"We've got to go. Quick!" He throws a bag at me. "Get your stuff."

When I ask him why, he won't look at me.

"Did you find her?"

He nods.

"Where is she?"

He takes his time, rubbing a heavy hand over his face. "She is dead, Oksana. In—in the canal."

1

Hope

"Well, all I can say is"—Mum sashays past me with a tray full of desserts—"I'm glad we didn't go for that little place in Languedoc. It's so much more *civilized* to be by the sea."

Dad grunts and makes some comment about Mum only being happy when she's near the stores, and everybody at the table laughs.

"I thought that's why you married me," she says, her voice deepening. "You needed someone to help you spend all that money!"

Another roar of laughter, the chink of glasses, scrape of knives and forks across plates.

I flick through the channels on the satellite box. Mum wanted me to join them like a polite and proper daughter, but they'll only talk about investments and property prices, and Mr. Crawley, who has the villa across the road, will give me these really sleazy looks when he thinks his wife's not paying attention. And I don't want to watch while Mum has a full-on geisha moment over Dad. It's like *so* pathetic it hurts.

Since Dad arrived, everything's changed. He flew in just for the week on Thursday, for the *last* week of our holiday. All the time we've been out here, Mum has been waiting for him to arrive, to find a "window" in his busy schedule for his annual family holiday in France. Now he's here, Mum is alive with gossip, business, new clothes. She's been planning this meal for weeks. She even ordered lobsters especially.

This is the third house they've bought over here. Dad says it's just another way of "managing wealth," but I think he does it to give Mum something to do while she waits for him. He's boasting to Mr. Crawley about how he sold the last one for a "healthy profit" and how European property is going the same way as the UK.

"The prices are stratospheric," he says, sounding pleased with himself. "Much better returns than the stock market."

When he showed up last Thursday in his new Armani jeans, his gray hair just buzzed, with his tennis rackets and water skis, smelling of sweat from the journey and free samples of Gucci Pour Homme, like the party was started now that he was here, I didn't want to talk to him, I wanted to punch him.

"Hello, princess." He tried to scoop me up in a hug, but I lay on the deck chair pretending to be asleep, my iPod throbbing in my ears. I waited for him to get off before I said hello.

We've hardly spoken since. I know he's disappointed that I won't play tennis with him, or go waterskiing. But I've been trying to make out like I'm not really bothered, just like he's not really bothered about us. There's a word for it: *nonchalance*— not concerned—it's a pose I've been practicing all holiday.

Next year I'll be nearly sixteen and officially too old to come out here anyway. I've already warned Mum that I'm staying at home after my exams. Or I might even go on holiday with my friends, Ibiza or something, like Kaz and Amanda were talking about.

Mum's not so sure. She gave me one of her "I'll deal with you later" looks when I told her, but she didn't start a fight. She was too busy flipping through curtain catalogs. She ordered hand-printed ones and had them shipped over here last week. All holiday she's been busy buying things.

"There's so much you need for a new kitchen," she said. But I can't see why she needs a rice cooker and an asparagus steamer and a coffee grinder, especially since we go out for meals most of the time.

I watch a repeat of *The OC* with the sound turned down. Out here cable is just the same as at home, except we get some weird French TV channels. Karen and Amanda were jealous when I told them I was going to our new house in the French Riviera for the summer, but they don't know how boring it is being here, even if there is a pool and the beach and a fifty-foot yacht.

"Imagine, all those fit Frenchies. You're *so* going to get it *on!*" Amanda rapped, wiggling her hips like Beyoncé.

But it's not all that around here. Most of the houses are owned by the English, and they're either retired, like Brian and Mavis Crawley, or professionals with young families like the Parry-Joneses. Mrs. Parry-Jones is a lawyer who looks stressed even in a bikini, harassed straggles of hair escaping around her face. They've got a villa on the other side of the hill, with no swimming pool, so Mum's been letting them use ours. This means I've been drafted in for babysitting the whole time they've been here. While Mum takes Mrs. Parry-Jones into Cannes for shopping, I get to look after Barry (eight) and Harris (ten) and watch they don't drown, while they dive-bomb the pool and play submarines.

There have been no fit men except, perhaps, Yves, the pool guy, who comes round once a week to dredge out leaves and hairs and other gross things from the pool filter. He's tall and tanned with black waxy hair and stubble. I've been practicing lying on the deck chair in my smallest bikini being *nonchalant* whenever he comes round.

5

Amanda says that if boys really like you they always ignore you. I think this is true of Yves. He goes a bit pink behind his ears whenever he sees me, and I've caught him staring at me, especially if he thinks I'm asleep. I wonder what it would be like if he came over and put his face close to mine and kissed me very, very gently on the lips.

I've spent the last month by the pool thinking about this, or wishing I was home in Norfolk, going to parties and hanging out. I've missed so much already. Amanda's been flirting with all these guys and Karen's got a new boyfriend. She sent me a photo on e-mail. He's twenty-three and drives an Audi TT and looks a little bit like David Beckham in profile.

When I go out with Kaz and Amanda men always come up to us. The minute we walk through the door sometimes. "Nice top, where you from?" Or, "I lost my phone number, can I have yours?"

Kaz and Amanda love the attention, it's obvious from the way they flirt and giggle. But I'm shyer. And, though I don't like to admit it, it makes me feel uncomfortable sometimes. I mean, I want to look sexy and beautiful and have men wink at me and tell me that I look great and all that, but when some of them hustle up close and press themselves against me it gets confusing, like they think I should let them feel me up, just because I'm having a conversation with them.

Mum thinks Karen and Amanda are low class because they are scholarship girls and Amanda's mum is a maid. But she doesn't have to go to school with the Norfolk county girls, all the Alexandras and Cassandras and Lavinias that Mum thinks I should be making friends with, girls whose parents have owned the English countryside for centuries. With their horsey faces and big blond dogs and Louis Vuitton school bags. Karen and Amanda are cool, because they're not like that. They don't seem to care if the whole school thinks they're ghetto, or that

6

they buy their school uniform at discount stores, or wear Burberry ripoffs from the market, or heeled ankle boots when they're supposed to have flat shoes.

Although she doesn't look it, Mum is kind of old-fashioned and overprotective. When I was born, she was nearly forty. Until she met my dad she thought she could never have children. "You were a miracle," she says when she tells the story of how I was born, and her eyes get big and watery. "I never wanted to let go of you. Not for a second." Now she's fifty-five, although people think she's younger. Last year Dad bought her a face-lift for her birthday and a new MG convertible. When she came back from hospital her face was bruised all over, like she'd been mugged.

They're talking about immigration now. Mr. Crawley goes on about how terrible it is, all these foreign workers showing up in Britain.

"We just don't have the capacity to cope."

There are murmurs of agreement. Then Dad says, "But on the other hand, I'm a businessman and I've got to admit, they do do all our dirty work. Cleaning, portering, building. No one in the West wants to do that sort of job anymore. They keep the economy going!"

"Bugger that polite claptrap!" Mr. Crawley bangs his fist on the table. I can see his expression through the wall, full of red wine and smug authority. "I mean, what are they *doing* here? Don't get me wrong, I'm not a racist, but I do object to people who have no right to be in this country taking jobs . . ."

"Darling, we're in *France*." Mrs. Crawley's voice sounds strained.

"Same difference. I'm all *for* Europe! It's all the illegal immigrants and asylum seekers that get me! I mean do you know how much of my tax money goes toward their social security? I don't pay tax so that some terrorists can claim housing benefit!"

There's silence for a moment, Dad slurps noisily on his wine. "In that case, the question I have for you is," Dad laughs to himself before he goes on, "how do you blindfold a Chinaman?"

"Derek!" Mum squeaks. "*Please*, we're not on the golf course now—"

"Use dental floss!"

And he and Mr. Crawley roar with laughter so loud that they can't hear Mavis and Mum muttering to each other as they clear away the plates.

In the morning Mum's in a mood. She's fussing around the house, grumbling about Dad and lack of decent storage space. I know she's still embarrassed about last night. Mum says it's the city that does it. That he's always rude and over the top when he's spent too much time in London.

"These French houses just aren't *designed* properly," she says, trying to squeeze another box of wineglasses into a full cupboard. "I mean, you need more than six cupboards in a kitchen."

She's already packed her Louis Vuitton cases. She says she's flying home and leaving me and Dad to strip the beds and do the vacuuming.

"I'm not suffering another journey in the Contraption," she says, pulling off her rubber gloves. "Anyway, we've got the new hot tub arriving at home and *someone* needs to be there while they install it."

"No! *Mum!* Can't I fly back with you? *Please?* It's not fair!"

I don't understand her. She spends all holiday waiting for him to arrive and then when he does, she can't wait to get away from him.

"Don't you start!" she says, suddenly aggressive, all angles with her elbows. Then, "Look, sweetheart, humor him, okay? Just this once? It means a lot to him to spend some time with you."

The Contraption is Dad's 1967 VW Camper van with all-original fittings. He spends most of what little spare time he has fiddling with it and adding new accessories, just so he can take photos of it for the enthusiasts' Web sites. He had it driven out here so he could drive it back home again himself.

Mum says she doesn't understand why he wants to drive about in a hippy mobile.

"For goodness sake! You're a *millionaire*! You can afford a *chauffeur*. I don't know why you're so obsessed with it."

But Dad says "the open road" is a classic British tradition.

"Well, why don't you just buy a Winnebago or something? At least that would have plush sofas."

When I was younger I used to quite like it: trundling along through the countryside like we're in some French movie. And it's cute the way you can pump water into the sink with your foot and boil water for tea on the minioven. But now the thought of spending all that time cooped up with Dad and no one else to talk to makes me feel weird and nervous and kind of annoyed.

"Mum, *please*."

But she won't budge. She tells me that it's good for us to spend some father-daughter time together. And she bribes me by promising I can stay over at Amanda's when I get back.

When the taxi comes she pecks Dad on the cheek—"See you later"—and hugs me—"You mind he doesn't crash it. And don't go talking to any strange boys on the ferry."

Then it's just me and Dad.

He clears his throat and looks at me out of the corner of his eye.

"So," he says. "So, what about those shutters?"

*

Once the sun has been shut out the house immediately starts to cool and the air starts to smell of earth and salt from the sea. When I go back outside the sun is blinding and I nearly walk right into Dad, who is talking to Yves in embarrassing French.

"*Garderez-vous un oeil sur l'endroit tandis que nous sommes partis?*" Dad says, pronouncing every word like he's got a phrasebook open in front of him.

"Er, yes, of course," Yves says, in English.

I try to go back into the house, but Yves is looking at me through his Ray-Ban sunglasses and smiling. Blood spreads up my neck and into my cheeks. "You will have no problems here. I wish you have a good journey. Bon voyage!"

Then he bends down and brushes his face against mine, once on each side, French style. He makes a soft kissing sound in each ear. "*Belle fille.*"

I can't believe it. In front of Dad and everything. My whole body goes stiff and my face is on fire. I clench my teeth and stare at his feet, noticing that even in blue pool shoes he looks cool. I want to sink through the floor.

"I'll be in touch," Dad says, shaking his hand.

When Yves has gone, schlepped the whole length of the garden in his slow, swinging walk, Dad looks at me and says, "I don't like that boy. He's a cheeky little sod."

"Why?" I ask, although I kind of already know.

"Never mind." He sucks his cheeks together. "Let's get the show on the road."

We've been droning through the hot yellow countryside for hours. I'm dripping with sweat even though we've got all the windows open, and now that the battery on my iPod has run down I've got to listen to Dad's hippy music—Cream and Fairport Convention—on worn-out cassettes that make the music sound slow and soupy.

There's been another heat wave in France this year. *La canicule* has been in the headlines of all the newspapers. The countryside around here is scorched, the grass brown and dying, trees already starting to shed their leaves. Lots of old people died, according to *Le Monde*, and now there's some scandal about them storing bodies in refrigerated trucks, because there's not enough room for them at the morgue.

"Disgusting," Mum said, and then, "Thank God for air conditioning."

Dad is uncomfortable, shifting in his seat, his face damp with sweat. He looks at me and sees that I'm twiddling my earphones round and round my fingers.

"Battery gone?"

I grunt.

Whenever we get in range, his mobile phone goes off like a Christmas display and he has to pull over and bark at people back in London: ". . . cash in those share options *now* . . . we need something liquid here . . . didn't we negotiate ninety-day terms? . . . can I count on you to set the ball rolling?"

Business conversations. He sounds like a boss then: tough, demanding. The sweat patches under his arms get darker.

We've achieved a kind of truce where if he doesn't ask dumb questions or crack racist jokes I don't give him dirty looks or pretend I can't hear him, but I'm still not going to get all father-daughter gooey over him. I slouch in the seat with my legs up on the dashboard, and stroke the fine nap of hairs on my knee that I missed when I was shaving. At least I got a tan.

He looks at me and coughs and allows a truck to overtake him. "So," he says. "So, how's your life?"

This seems like such a huge and random question. How's my life? What life? Last time I noticed I didn't really have one. I don't say this to him of course. Before I can think of an appropriate response he says, "Got your eye on anyone yet?"

11

"Um—"

"Only, you know, you need to be careful. In life. You know?"

"Not really." I look at him; he seems to be sweating even more.

"With guys, I mean men—boys—erm . . ."

"What about them?" He shifts about in his seat and leans over the steering wheel, staring at the road. I know what's coming. He's going to give me the "don't take sweets from strange boys" kind of speech, but I'm not going to make it easy for him.

"Well, now you're growing up a bit, people, *boys*, they start to notice you in a *different* kind of way."

"*Really?*" I try to sound innocent rather than ironic. "Like who?"

"You need to know that you don't have to do anything with anyone that you don't want to."

"Okay, Dad."

We whizz past a whole line of cars that are waiting at an intersection.

"And if you do find someone you think is really special, you feel free to introduce them to me. I mean I know I'm not around a lot, but I'm going to make it up to you, and—"

Yeah, right. He always says that. "Dad, I'm still a *virgin*. If that's what you want to know."

He makes a funny coughing sound. The line of cars starts to sound their horns at us.

"*Dad!* You're driving on the wrong side of the road."

"Oh." He brakes and swerves back into the right-hand lane. Cars have to move aside to let us back into the line. One man sticks his fingers up at us.

He changes the subject after that and puts Coldplay on the stereo. He tells me about the camper van, and how difficult it is to find parts, and then he goes on and on about the business and how easy it is to make money if you know how.

"Buy low, sell high," he says, as we creep along in the line for the ferry. "That's the first rule of business. And the second rule is don't be emotional. You want your customers to be emotional, but the businessman, he always has to be rational. That way, your customers will buy things because they *want* them, not because they *need* them."

2

Oksana

I could open the door and jump out. He forgot to lock it, he's so angry. Since we left Amsterdam he's been stopping every thirty miles to snort coke and that's made him talkative. He says he's got to take the rest of it before we get to Calais. Even with the air conditioning on he's sweating; the car is like a freezer although the computer on the dashboard says it's nearly 100 degrees outside. He drives as if it's a race, weaving in between the cars and trucks, speeding up, slowing down. Maybe if I'm lucky he'll have a heart attack before we get there.

He's stressed about Marie, he says. If the boss finds out what happened he's dead. And now there is only me, his profit margin is cut in half. He's practicing his story. He says he doesn't know what will come across best with the boss. That Marie ran away, or that a customer took her. "Perhaps we could find another girl?" he says, slowing down a little, scanning the passengers in all the cars we pass.

He says we have to go via France, because there's too much heat in Holland. Dead girls mean trouble, questions from the police, investigations.

"I mean it's not like I killed her!" he whines. "Silly bitch."

I think about Marie. I didn't really know her. We'd only been together for a week. Since Zergei brought me to Amsterdam. A tiny, skunky seventh-floor apartment right near the Oude

14

Kerk. She was already there when he pushed me into the room. She had long dark hair and dirty fingernails and she was too skinny. Her bones showed, like she was already dead, like her skeleton was trying to push out of her body. Looking at her made me feel a bit sick.

When Zergei came in with me she screamed and jumped away from him, flapping her arms and talking in some strange language, Romanian maybe. She didn't seem to speak any Russian and her English was really bad. A farm girl probably. Zergei told me he was pissed off with her; he said she needed to calm down. He had promised Nikolai *quality.*

"See if you can calm her down. Tell her this is a vacation. She doesn't have to work for a few days."

Then he threw my bag at me and walked out, double locking the door behind him.

She didn't seem to want to talk in any language. She lay on the bed looking at the wall, her hands together like she was praying. So I ignored her, tried to open the door a few times, tried the tiny letterbox window, too small to throw yourself out of. Maybe you could wriggle out of it, but by then you might have lost momentum and changed your mind. All around us there was noise: people talking, the thud of music from the bars downstairs, and the smells: the sharp scent of weed, greasy fries, beer, cigarettes, and the stink from the canals.

Sometimes she watched me, her knees drawn up to her chest. Her dark eyes took up her whole face. But even when I smiled at her she didn't respond. All that time she was watching and planning.

She picked the lock with a hairpin while I was sleeping. Ran out into the street and filled her hooded top with bricks, tied it around her waist and threw herself in the canal.

*

15

Zergei talks about his plan. He says that after the exchange, when they've given him the money, I should stay still and wait for him to come and get me.

"That is not a plan," I say. "How do I know you'll come and get me?"

"I *will*," he says, banging the steering wheel.

I know that this is not true. He's just trying to make himself feel better about what he's doing. He's not as cruel as Tommy. But I'm also not as stupid as I was back then. I know that men like Zergei don't know how to tell the truth. They only know how to watch their own back and it's really obvious that, right now, he's in trouble.

The road passes through fields of dead sunflowers, their heads hanging limp and brown, withering in the sun. I want to get away from here so bad it's like an ache in my stomach, but I can't move; even when he pulls off the road, hunching over to take more drugs, and I could just open the door and run. But where do I go? I've got no papers, no money and no clean clothes. And Zergei said once that if I ever tried to run away he'd fly back to my home town, before I could even figure out which way was north, and tell everyone what I was doing and what a dirty little bitch Oksana really was, so even if I did go home no one would want to speak to me anymore and anyway, he'd make sure that I was dead before I even got to the airport.

"I have contacts everywhere," he said.

Though I know now that this too is a lie—he's got no contacts, or else why did we have to leave Amsterdam so quickly when things went wrong? The big guys, the ones with real power, they employ men like Zergei to clean up for them. They don't get stuck on their own in Amsterdam with two girls they can't keep secure. Zergei isn't a boss man, he's just the delivery boy. He just does what he's told. He boasts to me, because he thinks I will believe him, but I've learned a lot about how to run a business in the last few months. More, probably, than I will need to know my whole life.

I have to get away from Zergei soon, before he takes me to London and makes the deal, but I need his help to get me into England first. I'm no good to Adik stuck in France. I have to go along with whatever Zergei says until we get across the water. I dig my nails into my palms and think of Adik. He better, better, better, damn well be there.

It wasn't always like this. Once I had a mother and father, somewhere warm to sleep: a family. Even in the winter, when it got so cold your spit froze before it touched the ground, there was always a glow in our apartment.

People gathered around my mother, they couldn't help themselves. When Adik broke his toe playing football only she knew how to make him lie still and stop his crying. And the way she would always remember everybody's birthdays and cook blini especially, even when there was not enough flour in the shops to make a small finger of bread.

All the time there was someone knocking on the door, wanting to borrow something, wanting to pay something back. She always knew someone who had just been paid, who owed her a loaf of bread, or someone who had been first in the line at the stores who had a spare piece of meat for a stew. She had a way of hiding things. And then forgetting where she'd put them, and then when she, or someone else, needed them most, she'd suddenly remember where they were. When everyone else was complaining because there was nothing except potatoes to eat, she would serve up *solyanka* and dumplings, still bubbling when she brought the pot to the table.

"My witch." That's what Father called her and he would slap her on the butt and laugh like he was pleased with himself.

I asked her once if she could do magic and she laughed.

"Of course," she said. "Every woman knows how to cook spells."

She was making cookies, her fingers nipping and pleating the pastry into spidery human shapes.

"Like *real* spells that can change people into frogs?" I thought of the stories she used to read me, of the prince who was turned into a frog, or of the witch in the woods who turned her hut into a gingerbread house just so she could tempt little children to her and eat them all up.

"I don't know that I'm very good at those kinds of spells," she said. "I haven't turned anyone into a toad for a long time. Tell you what, I'll make you a potion."

She shook some flour into a bowl and added a spoon of honey and some warm water. "Now I add the magic ingredient." She crumbled some yeast on top and stirred it. "Hubble hubble, make my potion bubble!" she said in a silly voice.

I looked at her and the bowl of floury water. "So?"

"You're disappointed, *kroshka*?"

"Nothing's happening."

"You have to watch, and wait."

"What will happen? Will it turn Adik into a frog?"

"No, *kroshka*, it will turn him very fat."

"*Cooool.*" I imagined Adik swelling up like a berry, and watched the floury water, waiting for a sign—a waft of blue smoke maybe, a dark and gooey farting.

"I can't see anything," I said after a minute.

"Hmmm." She looked at the mixture. "Look, see, it's bubbling." Small air bubbles were rising to the surface giving off a sweet, yeasty scent.

"It smells like bread," I said. "That's not *real* magic. That's not like turning water into wine." She'd recently been reading me Bible stories too.

"That was a miracle, *kroshka*, not magic."

"But what's the difference?"

She thought for a moment and then said, "Miracles, that's God magic. People magic, like in the story books, is not real, it's an *illusion*." She waved her floury hands around her body. "People magic is making people see what they *want* to see. And every woman knows how to do that," she added under her breath.

This still puzzled me. "So how is that"—I pointed at the bowl—"an illusion? How will it make Adik fat?"

"Oy!" She sighed and tweaked my ears. "You're like your father, aren't you? You always have to know everything *exactly*. Too many questions for today, *kroshka*, go outside and play."

I know she sees me now and can't bear to look at me. I see her in my dreams. Looking down at me, her face sad and disappointed. I know she can see all the things I have done since she died, and she's mad at me. I know I've let her down. That I deserve to be here.

Zergei says he has a new plan. He tells me, as we slow down to a stop in the line for the ferry, that he needs to find another girl. Any girl.

"How?!" I ask. "We can't just kidnap someone. People will see."

This is a stupid plan, a desperate plan. I look at him—his eyes are bulging in his head, his teeth are clamped, his nostrils red and flaring.

"No they won't," he says. He thinks it will be easy—after all, its not like we're really kidnapping someone. "We're just borrowing them," he says. "After I get my money I'll come and get you both. And she can go free. No harm done."

"But what if she screams? What if she tries to get away? What if she tells the police?"

He grits his teeth at me and stalls the car. I'm not sure how, because it's a brand-new Lexus. Then he gets in a mess with the gears and the car crunches and lurches forward.

"Now look what you did!" He grabs me around the wrist, crushing my bones in his huge hands. "Don't make me hurt you."

He says this a lot, usually before he's about to hit me. But it's not like I'm attached to him, forcing him to move like a puppet. He could let me go if he wanted—but instead, he's still trying to make out like he's doing me a favor. "I'm *helping* you, Oksana. Who are you without me? Eh?" He curls his lip and throws his arm back on my lap. "I'm watching you," he says.

One time, early on, in Italy, I tried to steal a cell phone. I thought maybe I could call home, tell Father to send some-one to come and get me. I got it out of his jacket pocket while the man was turned around, stepping into his pants. The phone was hot in my hand like a lump of burning coal, and my hands went suddenly heavy and slow. I couldn't hide it and when he turned, buttoning his shirt over his hairy belly, he saw it.

"Must have dropped it," he mumbled, looking at the carpet, darting out a hand to snatch back the phone.

Later, Antonio hit me. He said I should know better than to steal from customers. I would give him a bad reputation, get him closed down. I wouldn't look at him even when he was shouting. He kept calling me, "*Natasha, Natasha, you stupid, Natasha.*" Like that was my name.

After that I always tell them, whoever asks, that my name is Natasha, although Oksana is my real name. Natasha is who I am for them because Natasha is stupid and ugly and dirty. She's the one who got tricked, who thought life could be different, who wanted more than she deserved. Natasha is a nightmare, a bad dream of a life. Oksana is my real name.

3

Hope

I lean over the rail, and look at the thick spew of water that is churned by the engines of the boat. Dad's asleep in the first-class lounge, his complimentary copy of the *Telegraph* across his chest. We're on the *Berlioz* this time; on the way over it was the *Manet*. Mum thought it was really cheesy to name the ferries after famous French people.

"Honestly, these places are so tacky and full of the *worst* kinds of people." And she wrinkled her nose at a family that bustled past, hands full of milk shakes and bags of Big Macs.

She thinks that being rich should mean that we travel everywhere in *style*. "Well, what's the point of having money if you can't be *exclusive*?"

She's already phoned Dad three times to update him on the progress of the new hot tub. She's apparently mad because they've trampled through two flower beds getting the parts round the back of the house.

"Excuse me . . ." The voice has a weird Euro-English accent. "Do you have light?"

I turn round to face a thin girl in a denim jacket with dark, flat hair that's got streaks of orangey blond in it. Her skin is gray and pasty but her lipstick is the color of a post box or a fire engine. The contrast makes her look weird, like she's out

22

of focus. She puts her hands on her hips when I don't reply, and smirks.

"English? *Nederlands*? *Français*? *Italiano*?"

"Oh. English." I pass her my lighter, the one I bought in Cannes with a cannabis leaf on it. I've been hiding it from Mum all holiday. I bought it to show to Amanda, because her new boyfriend smokes.

She smiles and looks away as she takes it, which makes me feel nervous and reminds me of some of the older, meaner girls at school. The way they look when they're secretly laughing at you behind your back.

"Natasha," she says, blowing smoke as she speaks, "says thank you."

I shrug and wonder for a second why she talks about herself in third person. "Hope," I say.

"What is your name?" She pronounces each word precisely, like she's learned it from a teach-yourself CD.

"*Hope*," I say again.

"Oh!" Natasha laughs at her mistake, a sharp sound, like a dog's yap. She covers her mouth self-consciously. Her eyes dart from side to side all the time, keeping track of people coming out of the swing doors on to the deck. She bounces up and down on her feet like she's cold, the wind catching strands of her hair and blowing them into crazy shapes. "I am vacation in England," she says, grabbing the collar of her jacket and pulling it round her neck.

"*Going*," I say, "I think you mean you are *going on* holiday in England."

Natasha sucks her teeth. "Yes. I am *going* on vacation in England, where it is damn freaking cold!"

I laugh and ask her where she comes from. But she shakes her head and covers her mouth with her hand again. "I come from the world!" she says, curling the *r* in *world*. "Like you!"

"Well, no, *actually*, I come from somewhere quite particular . . ." and I begin to explain about our house, and Mum and Dad, and about living in the Norfolk countryside, and our holidays in France, but as I do her eyes glaze over like she doesn't understand, and I trail off.

"You have big house?"

"Well, I don't know. Compared to some people, I suppose we do, but not *that* big. I mean—"

"How many rooms?" she interrupts.

"Um, I've never really counted them before." I make a mental journey round our house. From the kitchen with the stable door and the TV room and the lounge and the dining room and the odd-shaped toilet under the stairs and the conservatory to upstairs and the three bedrooms and the bathroom and the library and then the study in the turret and the attic with another study and three more spooky rooms that are half furnished and full of books and Mum's old paintings and Dad's dusty boxes of papers from the business. "Um, sixteen." That sounds like quite a lot now I've said it and it doesn't even count the summer house and Mum's pottery studio.

"Are you famous?"

"No! My dad is a businessman. He sells—"

"I know what is a businessman." She shrugs and looks at the floor. "You have to go now. No more talking."

"Oh." I feel weirdly disappointed and a little paranoid. I still get the feeling she's kind of laughing at me. Then she points over my shoulder. "My boyfriend."

The man is standing close behind me. Too close. I wonder how long he's been there. He winks at me as I look and I don't know why. He's smoking, cupping the cigarette in his hand and, although he's smiling, his eyes are blank, expressionless. He's handsome and tanned, with black hair flecked with streaks of silver, and he's wearing designer clothes, Hilfiger jeans, an Armani top and K-Swiss sneakers.

Natasha runs over to him and grabs his hand. "We're get married," she says.

Getting, I think. You're *getting* married. But I don't say it aloud. "That's nice."

"You have to come to wedding! We're married in London!" Her voice is high and squeaky now, more childish than before and he's holding on to her hand so tight it's making her fingers white.

"Come now," the man says, his accent stronger, thicker than Natasha's. He lets go of her hand and grabs her arm. As they turn away from me, she mouths something at me that I can't make out. It isn't until they've disappeared into the crowds of children and families that I realize she's still got my lighter.

Inside, the boat is claustrophobic and stale. It smells of burgers and chips and chemicals from the toilets. I scan the rows of seats for Natasha and her boyfriend, but I can't see them anywhere.

The pitch of the boat is making me feel a little dizzy. I lie on one of the banquettes near the casino and look up at the gray ceiling tiles, although Mum told me if I felt seasick to look at the horizon. I switch on my mobile and check for a signal. But there are no new messages. I know that Kaz and Amanda must be out somewhere having fun without me and it makes me feel depressed and left out.

On the vehicle deck it stinks of gasoline and exhaust fumes. The sound of car doors slamming echoes off the metal walls, and as they open the back of the boat a cold sea breeze penetrates our thin summer clothes.

"Front or back?" Dad asks.

"Back," I say. I'm not in the mood for any more father-daughter chats.

Dad fiddles around trying to open the side door. "The lock's broken."

The people in the cars around us are watching, and the cars in front are already starting to move off. "Dad! We're causing a jam."

"I'm *trying*," Dad growls. Something gives and the door pops out and starts to slide on its runners. Dad stumbles and takes a breath. "There!" he says.

I climb in the back and Dad gets in the front. The cars behind are honking their horns at us. I sit on the sofa seat with the foam cushions that Dad had specially made with original 1960s material.

When I sit down something crunches. Dad must have filled the space under the seat with bags of duty-free.

One year, customs officers took the van apart. They went through all our stuff looking for drink and cigarettes. Dad stood with his hands in his pockets the whole time, jangling his loose change manically, his face going redder and redder.

"I'm not a drug smuggler! For God's sake! You officious little—" And then Mum had to shut him up because he started really swearing.

They fined him for having two more bottles of whiskey than he was allowed, which Dad reckoned was a "fix to stop me suing them for criminal damage."

As Dad starts the engine, the rustling noise gets louder, like there's something alive and wriggling underneath me. And then, as he carefully negotiates the ramp, a distinct cough which makes me jump up. Dad doesn't notice, all noise drowned out up front by the loud buzzing of the engine. When I look, there's a hand lifting up the cushion and . . . Natasha's face, holding a finger to her lips, signaling at me to shut up.

As the van emerges into daylight I have seconds to make a choice. If I say anything, Dad will hear me. I stare at Natasha. What's she *doing* here? How did she get in? And then I get this weird feeling that this is one of those moments where whatever decision I make, it's going to be the wrong one.

"*Please*," she whispers, "help me."

My heart starts to beat really fast. She looks very skinny and desperate, scrunched up with all our stuff. "Okay," I say.

She slides back into the pile of coats and duty free like a puppet going back into its box. I sit on top, as if she were never there. But I can still hear small, animal noises, the rustling of plastic bags, another little cough.

"Are you all right?" I hiss, putting my head between my knees so Dad can't see I'm talking. "Can you breathe?"

"What are you doing?" Dad says sharply, glancing at me over his shoulder. I straighten up. "Sit *still*. I don't want customs putting their grubby hands all over everything again."

I wonder what they'd do if they found Natasha. If they'd arrest us and everything. Maybe I ought to tell Dad. But it's too late, he's already winding down the window.

"Mind if we take a look in the back, sir?"

I freeze. I can feel all the blood draining out of my face. It seems to take ages for the customs official to open the door. I lie down and cover myself with a blanket.

When he slides open the door I blink at him, like I've just been sleeping.

"Uh?" I say, rubbing my eyes.

"Just routine." He puts his head through the gap. "Now you wouldn't have any hidden substances or illegal persons on a vehicle like this, would you?" He asks this like I'm six or something.

I can hear Natasha holding her breath. The silence crackles

like it's full of electricity. *Think of something to say, think of something to say.*

"I've just been sick."

The man's smile drops a little. "Oh."

I nod. "Really bad. Entrogastricitis or something."

"Gastroenteritis?"

"Yeah, that one. Mum reckons I got it off the water."

"Oh, dear." He hesitates for a second and then shuts the door and shouts, "All clear!" to one of his friends.

Dad starts laughing when we get out of range. "You're nothing if not my daughter." He shifts in his seat, sits up a little straighter. "That was quite a performance you put on in there."

It's starting to get dark as we turn out of Dover and begin the trundle home. My heart rate has just about returned to normal, although I still have a pain in my stomach. I move along the sofa seat so I can see out of the windows at the back, check there are no police behind us.

After we bypass Thetford I hear rustling again.

"Are you okay?" I whisper into the cushions.

There's more rustling and then a muffled voice. "*Shh.*"

I don't know what else to say. It's not like we can have a proper conversation. I wonder what to do when we get home. Dad will probably want to unpack the van right away, give it a once over before he goes to bed.

Mum accused him once of "loving that van more than you love me." He laughed at her when she said that. "Don't be silly, dear. This van is just a *symbol* of the things I love. How could I possibly replace *you* with an inanimate object?"

I suppose I ought to tell him, but I don't really want him to know. I don't trust him not to shout, or be embarrassing, or take her to the police right away. And I promised Natasha that I'd help her. If I can sneak her out of the van then maybe she won't want to hang around, although this idea makes me feel

28

noise in the bushes just ahead of me. "Go away! Leave me alone! I don't want you! Piss off!" It hisses.

"Well screw you too!" I shout at the bush, suddenly angry. And I stomp back up the drive to Mum.

When I was eleven I found a wildcat, trapped in a rabbit snare in the corner of the field next door. It was spring and I'd been dredging the shallow ditches at the edge of the fields for tadpoles with my net when I heard this noise that sounded like a crying baby. I searched through the grass until I found him, a cat with a dark gray coat, and tufts of hair on its ears which meant that it was wild. He was trying to get free but his back leg was broken and hanging at a sick angle. When I got closer he started to struggle, hissing and spitting, ears flat against his head. I stood quietly for ages, staring into space like I didn't care about him, all the while taking tiny, tiny steps toward him and making gentle cat sounds, and telling him stories about the rabbits he'd been chasing, and how bad it was to eat things that were as cute as rabbits, and how, if only he sat still for a second and let me help, then he could come home with me and have a nice tin of Whiskas.

But he was waiting for me. When I got close enough to touch his fur, he turned, yowling and spitting, baring a mouth full of sharp teeth, and he swiped me with his paw, making a big gash in the back of my hand. I've still got the scar, a white thread across the skin. I've never been so shocked in all my life and I ran home crying and smearing blood all over myself, so that Mum said she nearly fainted at the sight of me and had to take me to the hospital for stitches.

Dad phoned the farmer when he got home from work, and they went out together to look for it. When he came back, Dad was pale and he muttered something about the "barbarism of nature." I had to ask Mum later what had happened because he

31

wouldn't tell me. Apparently, the cat was so desperate to escape that it had bitten off its own leg and all that was left in the trap was a bloody stump of fur and bone.

"Don't think about it, dear, it will give you nightmares," Mum said, making me a hot cup of tea. But the thing is I wasn't disgusted. Round here you see dead animals all the time, roadkill at the junction to the main road—crushed rabbits, blackbirds, once a badger. And then there's the hunting season, men with guns and horses. Shooting pheasants and rabbits.

I wasn't horrified, I was disappointed. I wanted the cat to lie still so I could bring it home, pet it and make it better, and then it would be my friend.

4

Hope

From my bedroom window, all I can see for miles are the fields of barley and wheat, tall and golden, almost ready for cutting. Every year the farmer hires a combine harvester, which rips the grain from the top of the plant and bales all the stalks into straw for the animals. On windy days the air is full of dust and sharp stalks that get in your eyes and make you sneeze.

The farm is half a mile away through the fields. A low, medieval building; probably one of the oldest in the area. And round it are huge corrugated sheds crowded too close, like ugly brothers.

It's been a few hours since we got back and unpacked. She should be halfway to Norwich by now, if she's taken the right road. If she went across the fields, then she might just be walking herself round in circles, or have fallen in a ditch.

Mum and Dad are still up, talking. I can see the light under the door. It's hard to sneak out of this house without disturbing them, because their bedroom is right at the top of the stairs and because they don't sleep much anyway. It's one of the symptoms of being a relic, apparently: you need less sleep.

I check my mobile just in case Amanda's left a message. Nothing. I send her another text: *r u there? u still up 4 thurs? hx*

I put my fleece on over my pajamas, pull on a thick pair of walking socks and tiptoe out on to the landing. It seems strange

33

to be at home again after so long in France, like the house has grown and shrunk into a different shape while we've been away. I look at the stairs and try to remember which of the floorboards creak the loudest. There's a sigh and a click as their light goes out, plunging me into darkness. I hold my breath and try to let the banister take my weight so my feet are light on the stairs.

The back garden is outlined by the moon. I can't hear anything except the rustle of leaves in the poplar trees at the end of the garden, the plop and suck of frogs in the pond, an owl hooting gently in the oak trees across the field. And then I get this weird feeling that someone's watching as I walk up the path to the summer house, but there's no one there, just damp cushions and some of Mum's books, pages curling from the damp.

In the morning Amanda sends me a text message: *no can thurs pm. soz. have d8!!!! c u @ skool!! axx.*

This puts me in a bad mood before I even see Dad, pulling on his coat. I come down the stairs yawning, hugging my cardigan round myself.

"Bye, sleepyhead," he says, reaching out to ruffle my hair. I grunt and dodge out of the way. I wish he wouldn't talk to me like I was five.

He won't be back until the weekend now. The company has an apartment in London, where he can stay when he's working in town. Very occasionally Mum and I go up there for weekends to see Dad and catch a show or go shopping. I love it in London, the lights and the noise and all the stylish people, the sense that round every corner is a new possibility. It's not fair. I don't know why we can't live there.

"Suit yourself." He doesn't look at me as he pulls on his driving gloves. He opens his mouth like he's going to say something else, but then Mum comes out of the kitchen and clings on to him.

I hear the car revving while I wait for the toaster, and then I hear Mum, quietly closing the front door. The house always seems empty after he's gone. I shiver, and pull my cardigan tighter round myself.

After breakfast, I wander into the lane and search the hedge for clues—broken stems, crushed leaves, footprints in the mud. I find a little hollowed-out space in the hedgerow just past the beech tree. This is an old, gnarled tree with antique graffiti on it. Carved into the bark right at the bottom it says *Tray and Keren '77*. The branches have grown weird and twisted so it's easy to climb into them. When I was younger I used to climb up really high, leaping from branch to branch, right up into the canopy where the branches start to get thin and twiggy, and pretend I was a cat, or a bird. Thinking about this makes me squirm. Living here has made me really *lame*.

A bit further up, there's a foxhole in the hedge that you can squeeze through into the fields; here there's a thread of blue denim caught on the brambles. I climb through and follow the trampled grass round the edge of the field. And then I see her, knees drawn up to her chin, sitting in the long grass.

She doesn't look up, even when I get closer.

"Hello."

She doesn't reply. But I can see that she's shivering, denim jacket pulled tight round her. Her hair clings in dirty straggles to her neck and she looks younger than she did on the ferry.

"Are you all right?"

I put my hand on her shoulder and she jumps like I've hit her. But she doesn't say anything, chewing at the skin around her fingernails.

"Um, sorry." I don't know what to do then and stand there

35

looking at her, arms flapping uselessly against my sides. "I'm not going to tell anyone."

She stands up, shaking herself like a wet dog, hair flying. "You have food?"

"Well no, not on me, I mean, yes. At home." I don't know why, but talking to her makes me feel nervous.

"I want go to London." She says this like it's somehow my fault she's still here.

"Well you'll have to get a bus to Norwich and then a train."

"Nor-itch?"

"It's about twenty miles." I turn round and point through the hedge. "That way."

Her skin is gray and she's got panda eyes. She's rubbing her arms and stamping her feet, even though now the sun has burned through the haze it's starting to get quite hot.

"Do you want a jumper?"

"What is a jumper?" she asks, and then she laughs a rough sharp sound and starts jumping up and down. "I am a jumper!"

"Oh. I mean sweater." I laugh, but not because it's funny. I think she's really weird.

I fiddle with the cigarette packet in my pocket. I've only got one left and it'll take me ages to get some more. But her eyes light up when I pull the packet out of my pocket.

"D'you want to share?"

I spark the cigarette and take a short puff, passing it to her. She smokes it quickly, pulling the fire through the tobacco all the way down to the filter without passing it back.

"That was my last one," I say as she flips the butt into the field. "Don't do that! You could set fire to the field!" I crash down the bank, following the trajectory into the edge of the crops. The grass is already smoldering. I stamp at it with my foot. I tell her that this time of year, when the crops are really dry, it's easy to burn them. Especially closer to the main road.

One year the farmer lost two fields to a cigarette butt.

"You can't put it out," she says. I spin round, expecting to see that the fire has already caught the crops. "It's spreading."

"No, it's not." I trample the grass some more just in case.

"All over the whole world."

When I look at her, she's staring at the sky.

I'm annoyed now. She's weird, and I don't trust her.

"I'm going home."

She shrugs. "Yes."

But when I turn my back on her and start scrambling up the bank she follows me.

"What are you doing?"

"Coming with you." She smiles at me, which makes her whole face softer, more open.

"Make up your mind."

Instantly, the smile drops and her expression changes back into a blank scowl. "I go to London."

"Okay." I scramble through the gap in the hedge and jump down on to the road. "It's that way." I point up the lane and hurry away from her. Maybe I should call the police.

"Where is Tottenham?" She runs after me and grabs my arm. "You know? Where is Tottenham? Please?"

She sounds desperate again, like she did in the van. I don't know why, but I feel angry with her, like I want to fight her, and in the back of my head all I can hear is Mr. Crawley going on about how illegal immigrants are all criminals and terrorists. "Look. Just *calm down*, all right?"

As I raise my voice, her shoulders slump. "Natasha is sorry," she says, looking at her feet. Then she grabs my hand with both of hers. Squeezing, so I can feel the bones in her fingers. "Help me, *please* to find Tottenham."

I shake her off, but her hands are so cold and she just looks so desperate. I tell her that there are maps back at the house, but that she'll have to wait until Mum's gone out shopping. I tell her to stay hidden in the hedge, just for a while, and that I'll come back and get her when the coast is clear.

"Coast is clear? But we are not by the sea."

I stare at her. "Um, yeah, I know. It's kind of an expression."

"Expression?"

"Yeah. Don't worry about it. I'll come back in a while."

"Okay." She smiles at me again. "You are *friends* to Natasha?" And she scurries back through the hole in the hedge.

Mum is in the garden, deadheading the flowers, clipping back the greenery. Shaping the plants so they grow the *right* way. She's got her floppy sun hat on, a big white crocheted one that she bought for a wedding in the seventies.

"Hello, child," she says as I sidle up to her.

"Mu-um?"

"Yes, dear?"

"We haven't got any food."

"Don't be silly, there's lots of food. Just defrost something from the freezer." Mum always keeps leftovers in plastic bags in the freezer. Small dollops of meat sauce, or curry or soup, but they go funny after being in the freezer and taste like sick. I tell her this, but she just gives me one of her looks.

"I'll go to the stores when I am good and ready. It's not like you're starving, is it? I've offered you some food, it's not *my* fault if you don't like it."

"Well it's not *my* fault that I've got bad parents," I throw back at her, suddenly annoyed.

Mum is really paranoid about being a bad parent. She thinks, because she had me so late, that she wasn't really "one of life's natural mothers." Maybe that's why she treats me like a cross between her granddaughter and an irritating fly.

About ten minutes later she comes back inside the house,

dumping a basket of lavender on the kitchen table. She changes out of her gardening shoes and winds the car keys round her finger. I'm making a big deal of ignoring her, cuddled up on the couch, pretending to read.

"You ready then?" she says eventually.

"I'm not coming."

"I thought you said you were hungry."

"I'm reading my book."

She sighs and taps her foot. "You know, when they told me that the teenage years were the worst part of being a parent, I didn't believe them. Silly me. I don't understand why everything with you has to be an *argument*. Can't we just get along like a normal family?"

This makes me snort. A *normal* family? "Normal families don't live in the middle of *nowhere*."

She gives me one of her looks. A you're-not-really-my-daughter kind of look.

"You don't know how lucky you are, young lady." She pinches my ear nearly hard enough to hurt.

"Child abuser," I say, swatting her hand away.

When she's gone I take Natasha round the back, through the conservatory, which is like a minijungle of pot plants and orchids. She doesn't say anything as we go through into the kitchen, but she touches everything with her fingers. Gently running them over the units, the dishes piled up on the sideboard, the kettle, the toaster.

"You have much moneys," she says quietly.

"Not really. I mean, Mum and Dad have lived here since I was born. I mean, they hardly paid anything for the house when they bought it."

She looks blank, like she doesn't understand what I'm saying. I get some cheese and crackers and put them on a plate.

"Where are you from?"

She shovels in cheese and crackers, spraying crumbs all over the floor.

"Ngh," she says with her mouth full. She swallows and starts coughing. "I have to go to Tottenham. Show me where is Tottenham."

"Okay. Okay." I rummage through the bookshelf on the dresser where Mum keeps all the maps and bills and cookbooks. "Is that where you're getting married then? Tottenham?"

"Married?" She looks puzzled for a second, then her face changes and she starts laughing. "I don't get married."

"But you said—"

"That was yesterday." She shakes her head. "And now it is today! Now is another story!" She smiles, quick, sharp; not like the kind of smile you give people when you're happy. She looks away from me at her hand, and pauses over a gold ring on her wedding finger. She pulls it off and gives it to me. "Here. To pay." She points at the empty plate.

"Oh, no!" I push her hand away but she puts the ring on the table and shrugs.

It's then that I notice she's got dirt on her face and her thin, skintight trousers are covered in muddy marks from the fields and she kind of *smells*; and then I realize, although I've noticed it before I never really thought about it till now, that she's got no stuff. No bag or anything, or any clean clothes.

But before I can ask her more questions there's the crunch of gravel in the drive and the sound of an engine running. I peek out of the window to see the car parked nearly in a flower-bed and Mum getting out of the driver's seat. She's calling my name.

"Quick!" I grab Natasha's hand. "Hide!"

We sprint upstairs and into my bedroom. "Stay in here.

I'll get rid of her. She's probably just forgotten her purse or something."

"Hope! Hope! Darling?! Are you there?" She sounds out of breath.

I'm back downstairs and into the kitchen just in time. "Why didn't you answer me the first time?" She's got her hand pressed over her chest like a lady in an old-fashioned painting.

"I was reading." I hold out the book, and realize I've been pretending to read it upside down. But she doesn't notice.

"Don't *do* that to me. I didn't know what—I thought—" She catches her breath.

"Did you forget your purse?"

"No. I forgot *you*. You're coming with me. *Now*." Her face is pale, shocked.

"Why? Where are we going? What's happened?" My chest tightens; she sounds scared and serious.

"I'll tell you in the car."

"But—"

"No buts."

Before we leave she checks that all the doors and windows in the kitchen are locked. "You haven't seen anybody around the place this morning have you?"

"No!" My face freezes—how does she *know*?

She bolts the door into the conservatory, grabs my arm and hustles me out of the house. She double locks the front door behind us, pauses on the front step and looks out over the fields. The morning swallows are already high above us, cutting through the air, making sharp razor calls.

"Can you see anything?"

"What am I supposed to be looking for?" The fields, sewn together by thick hedges and lines of poplar trees, all look the same as usual to me.

"Anything out of the ordinary."

She never locks up like this unless we're going on holiday. Sometimes she even leaves everything completely unlocked when we go shopping.

As I get in the car she tells me that she's sorry, but it's not safe to leave me on my own. "Not today." The tires screech as she wrenches the gears and the car bounces out of the drive into the lane, narrowly missing the gatepost. I look up at the house and I'm sure I can see movement, a flutter of the curtain in the front bedroom, the shadow of a person behind the glass.

"There's been a break-in, at the farm. Only they didn't take anything. Just turned the place upside down. Like they were looking for something apparently. Yesterday night, while the family was all in the pub, just after we got back."

My fingers tingle with relief. She doesn't know about Natasha. It's just a stupid burglary.

"Probably kids," Mum says, "but I don't want to risk leaving you on your own." She says there have been a few sightings since, a strange car parked in the lane, a man in a leather jacket seen running across the fields.

My heart starts beating fast and loud. Natasha's boyfriend had a leather jacket.

"Mum—" *I met this girl* . . . The words form on my lips but I don't say them. What if all this has nothing to do with Natasha? And anyway, I don't know why, but I can't tell Mum about her, not yet. What I do know is that since yesterday, when we got off the ferry, the air has had a weird, exciting fizz about it, a crackle of static like the electricity in the air before a storm.

5

Oksana

The English girl has more clothes than I have seen, even in the stores. When I open the wardrobe door some of them tumble out all over the floor. Rolled up tops and jeans, skirts and dresses, jackets that have lost their hangers.

I don't know where she's gone. Her mother came to get her and her voice was sharp and scared. My heart is really beating now. He's here. I know he is. I can smell him, the greasy hair, the sweat, the Hugo Boss aftershave that makes him think he's a player. But maybe I'm just being paranoid.

I have to get away from here, and *quick*. I need money and clothes. I can't stop to think again. I'll get stuck, staring at the fields and the birds, not wanting to move. The English girl already thinks I'm crazy, I can tell. I grab a pair of jeans and a few T-shirts. They look expensive and new. When I've found Adik, I'll send her some money. I'm not a thief.

I grab a green bag with a red badge on it, Manhattan Portage. I try to stop my hands from trembling as I stuff it with clothes. I need money. Enough for a train fare at least. But I don't know how much English pounds are worth. In Italy they always paid in euros. So much cleaner than roubles; the notes in euros were always new. Not worn and dirty like at home, where everyone worries about the notes in their hands, wishing they would grow into more or change by magic into dollars.

Not that I ever kept any of it. Zergei, and before him Antonio, always took it away from me straight afterward—before I could count it.

Where do English people keep their money? I lift up the mattress but there's nothing there but an old sock. I look around her room; all over the surfaces there is stuff. Jewelry, makeup—I put a lipstick in my bag—on the walls there are posters of models and films stars. I open a drawer and find some coins, a few that say one pound, which I know is worth more than the brown pennies. Five pounds. I don't know if that's enough. Somehow I don't think so. Zergei grumbled to me once that it was expensive to live in London.

The house is so big I don't know where to start. There are two more bedrooms on this floor, one of them empty, just a blue bedspread over the huge bed and expensive looking lamps. Everything *smells* rich: clean and new. I know I could sell this stuff back home, Tetya Svetlana would be falling over herself to get these bedspreads, the curtains, the lamps. There's more *quality* in this empty room than Zergei could ever dream of.

He was getting crazy on the ferry. The drugs, maybe the stress, I don't care. He said he would throw me off the boat if I screamed, and held me round the throat so I couldn't breathe. For a second I thought he would kill me, right there on the back of the boat with all the people smoking their cigarettes. Although, I am much smaller than him and he was hiding me with his body. Anyone who looked might have thought he was kissing me.

"You let her *go!*" he said, his eyes popping. "I told you the plan!"

I was supposed to make friends with the English girl and take her to look at the car or something stupid like that. Then he was going to push her into the car and take her off the ferry and through customs using Marie's passport.

"She doesn't even look like Marie!" I said. "She'll shout!"

He didn't like me pointing out flaws in his plan. "Shut up and do it!"

But when it came to the moment she was so stupid and sweet and innocent I couldn't. Even with Zergei standing behind her. I knew he wouldn't do anything himself. It was too risky. He couldn't just kidnap someone in plain daylight. People would see.

When they made the call to get back to the cars and he was still standing in line for cigarettes, I ran. My heart beating so fast I thought I might pass out or fall over. My legs seemed like they weren't there, like they were made of feathers, or air.

"Hey!" And I heard him shouting my name down the stair-well. "Hey!"

I had seconds; all the families were coming back to their cars. I had to find somewhere good, somewhere no one would ever look. I heard a story once about a boy who came to Italy by holding on to the underside of a truck all the way from Vienna, but I was on the wrong deck for trucks, I was with the family cars and caravans.

At the time it seemed weird that I picked her van. Like a good sign. But now I think it was the worst idea I could have had. He must have seen me when I broke open the door, and it would be easy to follow. It got me through the border, but I don't know if it got me away from *him*.

The house is so huge and comfortable it's like a movie star home from the magazines. The carpets are as thick as snow.

I tiptoe even though I know there's no one to hear me. In the kitchen I open all the drawers. Maybe I could sell some of the knives and forks, or the thick cotton cloths—I could carry those in a bag. Then I find what I am looking for: sticking out of an envelope hidden underneath some folded material. Four twenty-pound notes: eighty pounds. It looks like more money than coins. I stuff it into my back pocket and shut the drawer. Adik will help me find a better job, a real job, so I can pay it back.

I pull the corner of the postcard with Adik's address on it out of the padding of my bra. Twisted up like a candy wrapper. The card was a collage of London with soldiers in red coats and tall fur hats, and gray palaces and a big wheel. Even though I know it by heart I have to look, to remind myself that it's real: 88 Lordship Road, Tottenham, London.

The postcard just said—*Write me. Adik xx.* And the address. I took it with me when I packed, just in case. Tommy said I would get a break in between jobs and, sure, I'd get plenty of opportunity to travel. When he told me this I was so excited. I imagined how surprised Adik would be when I showed up. *Hey, it's me. Guess what? I couldn't wait. I got a job too.*

Now I can't think of Tommy without his face twisting in my mind. The sneering look he gave me when I started crying and told him I wanted to go home. And I remember Antonio saying I was a stupid girl, that of course Tommy had explained to me what I was supposed to do before he sent me to him in Italy— I just wasn't *listening* properly.

I wonder for a second what I will do if Adik isn't there. But I can't imagine that. The only thing that is keeping the blood flowing in my body is the thought that he will be there. He will be there to call me Oksana, to remind me who I am.

I grab a few apples and bananas from the bowl in the kitchen. I will get a job. Whatever it is, I don't care, as long as it's not sex. I am still strong, I can work kitchens, I can work factories. Anything.

Just when I'm ready to leave, I see the phone on the side by the fridge. Like a white walkie-talkie that policemen use. The idea of calling home is suddenly so close it makes me feel ill. I could let Father know I am still alive. Tell little Viktor about the million bucks house and the movie-star living room.

When I dial in the numbers nothing happens. Just a flat tone. I try again and get the same. I put it down, disappointed, and stare at the smooth expensive plastic. Maybe I need to dial an operator number first. There is only one phone in our block. At the bottom of the stairs, on the other side from our apartment. You have to buy phone cards from the store to use it. Maybe it's out of order again.

There's a telephone directory under the table. I flick through the pages but the English looks dense and heavy and I have to concentrate to see words I can read. I make out the word Russia and a code. I dial the code and then our number again and there's a hiss and a few clicks and then a soft purr. It seems to ring forever before someone picks up.

"Hello?" I don't recognize the voice.

"Er, it's Oksana Droski. I'm phoning for Tolya in apartment sixty-three."

"Who?"

"Tolya Droski and Viktor in apartment sixty-three."

"They moved out," she says.

"Oh." My heart is suddenly full of lead. "Do you know where? Did they leave an address?"

The woman sighs. "Hold on."

More crackly static, then feet shuffling against concrete, the sound of someone knocking on a door and then voices, but I can't make out what they're saying. *Moved out?* My heart sinks. All this time I imagined Viktor going to school, playing football in the courtyard. And now they've gone someplace without me. I feel like I want to throw up. All over the thick carpet and soft sofa and million bucks house.

"Hello?"

"Are you the whore?"

"What?!"

"Oksana Droski, Polina and Tolya Droski's daughter. You ran away to become a whore."

A hot flush of shame courses through my body. I don't know what to say. Zergei used to say if I ran away he'd tell everyone back home what I was. "Then they won't talk to you anymore." But it seems like the secret was already out. My heart freezes over at the thought that Father knows.

"Mrs. Shiroff says they went to Moscow to live with Polina's sister. I don't know where."

"Oh."

"Mrs. Shiroff says you never sent any money. Even Mrs. Shiroff's daughter sends money."

"I'm not a whore! You don't even know me!" I shout. I wonder who it is that told them.

"We all have a difficult life," she says, and hangs up.

I drop the phone as I'm trying to put it back in its cradle. The plastic cracks apart like a nutshell, spilling out guts made of wire and batteries. I bend down to try to put it back together but my hands won't work properly. Gone to Moscow? Without waiting for me? How long have I been away? I try to count the months, fourteen, perhaps fifteen. I don't understand. Maybe they thought I was dead. I throw the phone back on the floor and stamp on the pieces.

6

Hope

Everyone in the store is talking about it. Deborah, the cashier, is waving her hands around like she saw it all herself.

". . . and the shock of it—all the cups and plates broken into pieces and everything. I mean, what's the point in that?"

A group of old ladies from the village stands around the cash register making oohing noises. Like pigeons, I think, as Mum distractedly fills her basket with three packets of crackers.

"Mum . . ." I grab her sleeve, "you've got three . . ."

"Shhhh." She shrugs me off, still listening.

". . . well, I think it was drugs, that's what made them do it." Deborah folds her arms over her green apron. "People do crazy things. That's seven ninety-eight, please, love."

"Cheddar or Brie?" Mum picks out a triangle of cheap Brie and turns up her nose at the brand. "The selection here is so *poor*," she hisses at me.

"Whatever," I shrug, trying to hide in the bakery aisle and pretend like I'm not with her.

"Really, Hope, do you have to slouch like that?" She gives me one of her looks, like she wishes that she had another kind of daughter, the kind who has good posture and holds her knife and fork properly and is polite and makes interesting conversation with her parents.

"Well, I suppose it doesn't matter if you're not the sharpest knife in the drawer. I mean, we can't all be blessed with the

49

brains of your father," she said to me once after I got okay, but less than fantastic, results on my SATs.

"Are we going to be here all day?" I ask, turning my nose up at the vegetarian pâté in their new "Deli-icious" range that she has put in her basket.

"It's *you* who wanted lunch."

The women at the counter shuffle out of the way for Mum.

"I heard about the farm," Mum says to them.

And then they're off, repeating the story again, like we haven't already heard it twice going round the store. This time there are new details. Kevin, the farmer's son, has bad debts they think. Too fond of his poker, might be someone he owes has done him over, for revenge, like. Because it seems strange for an attempted burglary. What's the point of smashing stuff up before you steal it?

I try to pretend I'm not there. The minutes tick by like hours on the Silk Cut clock behind the counter. I worry about Natasha locked in the house. I don't know why but I am worried about her. I want to get home and check that she's still there.

Back in the car, Mum seems reassured, but she's still freaked out that she hasn't been able to get hold of Dad. "He's had his phone on voicemail *all* day." Mum always seems to think that Dad should be there for her, instantly, just when she needs him.

"Maybe he's busy," I say tiredly.

"Hmm. He's always busy in a crisis."

The moment we get back home I run upstairs, pretending to Mum I need the bathroom. My bedroom is warm like someone has been in it, but she's not there.

I feel sort of disappointed, then paranoid that she might be somewhere else in the house, where Mum can find her.

Suddenly there's a crash in the wardrobe that makes me jump, some muffled swearing. Then the doors swing open.

Natasha kind of falls out of it with my clothes and all the hangers and a broken clothes rail on top of her.

"Shit!"

I giggle because it's funny and I'm nervous. But she doesn't look very amused.

"Why do you lock the doors? Natasha couldn't get out!" She sits up, throwing my jacket off her head. "Now your wardrobe is breaking!" Then it's like she sees me laughing and can't help giggling too. "I thought it was your mother."

She stands up, brushing dust off her clothes and smoothing her hair flat. She half smiles at me, like I'm amusing but annoying, something to be tolerated.

"Are you, like, in trouble or something?" I ask her.

She turns away from me and folds her arms. "Why you always want to know what I am doing? Why you always asking? Blah blah blah, all the time. I don't *want* to talk about it! Always talking! If I want to do talking then I *tell* you! Anyway, I have to go. *Now*."

She gets up and bounces like she needs to pee. I can hear Mum in the kitchen, rattling cups in the sink. She'll want me downstairs soon.

"You'll have to *wait*." I try to explain to her that if Mum sees her she'll call the police, but she just hears the word "police" and her eyes widen.

"No *policija*! No police!"

"It's okay. It's okay. There's no police here. *Promise*. Wait until I go downstairs, and then you can go. Out the front, okay, and don't go past the kitchen or Mum will see you."

She grabs my hand and says thank you and then lots of things in a weird language that I don't understand, which sounds like maybe it could be Russian. All I can think is how cold and bony her fingers are, and how tightly she's holding on to me, and I don't know why, but I don't want her to leave.

An idea blooms in my mind, a plan. It comes so fully formed, that I know it must be the right thing to do.

"If we leave really early I can be there and back in a day. And I'll leave a note so Mum won't call the police. It won't take long to find Tottenham on the map. Not once we're in London. And I've still got money left over from Christmas, in my account maybe a hundred pounds, enough to get us there. I'll take you. I'll *show* you!"

Natasha closes one eye and kind of squints at me. "You coming with me? To Tottenham?"

I nod. It's not like I've got anything else planned. And then I can tell Amanda I went to London, never mind about her missing a night out on Thursday for a stupid date.

She laughs. "You want to come with me?!" Then she shrugs. "Okay. If you want."

I tell Natasha my plan. She will go downstairs and out the front door while I distract Mum, and then she'll have to hide in the summer house until it gets dark. When Mum is asleep, I'll join her and we'll get the really early bus to Norwich, the one that goes at six from the bus stop at the end of the lane.

When I walk into the kitchen I am weak with nerves. My senses are so intense I'm sure I can feel even the slightest breath of air against my skin. Mum's bustling. Cleaning surfaces, clattering plates.

"Your father thinks it's nothing to worry about." She sounds annoyed about this.

"Oh."

"You know, Hope, when you find a man, make sure he's someone you can share your life with." She scrubs a scouring pad round the sink; the scratch of metal makes my teeth hurt. I never thought she could see me with a man before; that's new.

"Are you going to split up with Dad again?"

Before she had me, Mum had a job with an insurance company, her own office, a secretary. Then Dad got rich and suddenly there was no need to go back to work.

She turns to me and puts her hands on her hips. "How would it be if we moved into the city for a while, just you and me?"

"Um . . ." I can hear a creak on the stairs, Natasha's shadow passes across the door to the hallway. "Yeah, *cool*."

Mum says this every time she's in a mood with Dad, but when it comes to the moment, she can never leave. She got as far as the front door once, suitcases packed, me in my coat with a rucksack, but when she got to the door she started crying. "I just couldn't do it. I looked at that umbrella rack, the antique one we got for a wedding present, and I couldn't bear the thought of leaving."

"You know, we could get a little house in Norwich or something if I can force your father to sell this place."

The latch on the front door clicks softly, too soft for Mum to hear, and Natasha's out of reach.

"It's typical of him to abandon us in a crisis. I need him to come home tonight, after everything that's happened today."

She goes on like this until she runs out of words and then she changes the subject. "Darling? Have you seen the downstairs phone? It seems to have disappeared."

I wait half an hour after Mum's gone to bed, watching out of the bedroom window with the lights turned off. In the moonlight, the summer house looks like a face: the shuttered windows half-closed eyes, the circular decking a gaping, toothy grin. I blink, to make the image go away. I hope Natasha's still out there.

Snuggling into my coat I check my room, in case I've forgotten something important. I've got my bank card, a map of London, my phone. I pick up a strawberry lip balm and a pound coin and put them in my pocket. Twelve fifteen. Another ten minutes and I'll go outside. As I watch, I'm sure I can hear a low grumbling in the lane, the crunch of feet on gravel. I open the window wider to try and hear. Think maybe it's Dad, coming home early after all Mum's phone calls. But the air is silent, thick and damp from the heat. Nothing.

A shape appears, escaping from the side of the summer house, no more than a shadow, disappearing into the bushes with a soft crackle of greenery. *Natasha*. She's heading toward the hedge—the only place she can go from there is into the cornfield.

My hands fumble as I unlock the back door. I can't do it quickly enough. I run through what this might mean, feeling stupid, betrayed.

"*Natasha?*" The undergrowth nearby rustles. I step off the path into the borders, my feet sinking into the soft piles of mulch Mum heaps around the plants. She'll go mad if I tread on anything, but I can't think about that now. The rustling backs away from me toward the hedge.

"Natasha? What's going on?"

"Shhhhhh." A hand grabs me and pulls me back toward the fence into a noisy thicket of bamboo. She puts a sticky hand across my mouth. "Shhhh, *please*."

I crouch down beside her and hold my breath, the garden is suddenly loud with sound. Something rustles in the bushes —a rat, a mouse, maybe even a rabbit, scrabbling about in the undergrowth by the greenhouse; our bodies tremble in the grass.

"He's *here*," she whispers.

"Who?"

She doesn't answer, but when I look at her, her eyes are wide and wild again.

He seems to come from nowhere. Suddenly, there's this man standing in front of us and he seems much bigger and taller than he did on the ferry.

7

Hope

It's hard to know what happens next. I am aware of being pulled up by the arm, and Natasha screaming and trying to run away, but he's got her too, held off the ground, arm round her neck. I kick, but my feet are only scuffing the top of the grass, and the body that's carrying me grunts as he crosses the lawn.

For a moment I am too stunned to react. Where did he come from? How come I didn't see him? Then I scream, call out for Mum, loud enough to make him shake me.

"Shut up!" he says, voice dark, foreign. "Stupid girls."

And then we're in the lane, next to a dark Lexus with blacked-out windows. He drops me so he can open the trunk, and I know I should run, but it takes ages for the thought to reach through the panic to my legs, and by the time my muscles have reacted, he's got hold of me again.

"Get in," he says, pointing at the dark space of the trunk. Natasha obediently bows her head and clambers inside, curling up her body to fit herself in the space.

"No way!" I struggle against him, but he's solid, muscled, like a bodybuilder. He tightens his grip on my arm, squashing muscle against bone. "You're hurting me!"

If I can stall him long enough maybe Mum will hear me screaming. I manage a kick against his knees that makes him yelp and buckle for a second, but he doesn't let go, and suddenly I'm lifted and tossed into the trunk of the car like I'm a doll. I land heavily, half on my elbow, half on top of Natasha. He grabs my bag off my shoulder then he shuts the lid with a slam, plunging us into total darkness.

I can hear someone screaming and it takes a moment to realize that it's me. Natasha wriggles to get her legs out from underneath me. I go to sit up, but my forehead collides with metal.

Natasha's pulls me down next to her so I'm lying on my side.

"Lie down," she says. "It's easier."

"*Easier?*"

And then he starts the car.

The roar of the engine is close and deafening and as the car shoots forward we're bounced up and down over every pothole in the lane.

"Let me out!" I shout so loud my throat hurts. "Let me out!"

"*Shhhhhh.*" Natasha puts a hand across my mouth, her skin is clammy and smells metallic, like she's been holding money. "Do you want him to tie you up and gag you?"

The car slows and turns, and then I know we're out on the road, the engine is smoother, faster, the road close underneath us. Already it's starting to get hot and it stinks of gasoline.

"I can't breathe."

"*Sleep,*" Natasha says. She's curled up behind me, pressed right back into the hollow of the trunk.

"I don't *want* to sleep. I want to GET OUT OF HERE!" I shout, turning round so I'm facing her, but it's no good, it's too dark to even see my hand in front of my face. I reach out and grab at her until I've got hold of an arm. "Where are we going?!" If he's going to kill me I think I should know about it.

She doesn't answer.

"TELL ME!" I want to punch her until she disappears and I wake up in bed at home. I pinch her arm.

"Ow!" She fights me away with her hands. "Leave me alone!"

The car lurches and a horn beeps. My stomach hurts and I'm starting to feel sick.

"Where are we going? Tell me." I try to kick her, but there's something in the way. A box or a spare tire, I can't tell. "*Where?*"

"I don't know." Natasha hiccups and I realize she might be crying, but it's too dark to know for sure. "Maybe London."

My mouth is dry.

"Why? Why does he want us?" Then the car begins to slow down, I can hear the sound of other vehicles. Traffic lights.

"HELP! HELP!" I bang the side of the car. "HELP!"

I want to get out of here so bad it's like my blood is trying to burst out of my body.

Natasha's really crying now, making snivelling snotty noises. I can't even sit a little way up without banging my forehead. This is what it's like to be buried, I think.

"This is all your fault!" That's all I can think. *All your fault.* I should have trusted my instincts. I should have told Mum about her.

She grabs me, clumsily, then tightly, round the wrist.

"He wants Natasha. Not you," she says.

"HELP!" I kick my feet. If I make enough noise maybe someone will hear, and stop him. "HELP!"

"*Shhhhh.* Really."

The car speeds up again, racing off the lights, taking my stomach with it. The smell of rubber and gasoline and no air, Natasha's sticky hands and the panic and the outrage all slosh around my body.

I turn my head away from her just in time.

Natasha strokes my head and pulls my hair away from my face.

"Breathe slow," she says. But I can't stop. Now all I can smell is my own vomit, sharp and thick.

"This is how it was with me, the first time. When they took me to Italy. I was in the car for two whole days. Much better to sleep."

"Are they taking us to Italy?!"

"I don't think so." She wriggles around next to me and gives me a cloth of some kind. "Here, for you to clean."

"What's this?"

"Your T-shirt."

"You took my stuff?"

"I was just to borrow it." She hands me a fat bundle. "You can have it back now."

"You have to tell me." Throwing up seems to have cleared my head, but I can't stop my teeth from chattering. "You have to tell me, Natasha. You have to tell me what's going on. What does he want? I thought he was your *boy*friend?"

I know she's been lying about him, just like I knew Kaz was lying when she brought a photo of her cousin to school and pretended like she was going out with him.

"I mean, boyfriends don't throw you in the trunk of their car and drive off!"

"He wants me because I run away from him," she says eventually, her voice barely a whisper over the snarl of the engine. "He said if I run away he will drive down every road in every country until he finds me."

"Why?!"

I'm not sure I hear the next bit right because she's wriggling around, turning her body away from me, the bones of her spine pressing through her clothes and against my arm. "Because he *paid* for me."

"Paid for you?! How did he pay for you?"

No one buys people anymore, they banned that, we did it in history. And anyway, it was only people from Africa, it wasn't like, *white* people. William Wilberry or something, or maybe it was Wilberforce, who banned it. I wasn't really listening because Kaz had brought her mobile into class and was taking sneaky photos up her skirt to send to her new boyfriend.

"No talking," she says. "Natasha sleeps now."

"But—" My mind fizzes with uneasy questions. *Paid for her?* I don't get it. Why would anyone want to buy a *person*? And I don't understand what that's got to do with me. Why does he want me?

"Well, he hasn't paid for *me*."

It's hard to know how long we've been on the road. The car drones on and on and I must fall asleep, because I wake up suddenly, gasping for air, my mouth dry, head aching. For a second I convince myself that I'm dreaming, trapped in the middle of a long nightmare, and Mum will come in soon and switch on the light and tell me I've been shouting in my sleep. I pinch myself hard on the leg, just in case.

The car swerves and suddenly slows down. We are thrown forward together. I catch my arm on a screw or something and it scrapes a flap of skin off my elbow.

"Ow!"

I wonder where we are. Maybe if we're quick enough we could escape when he stops. Spring out and surprise him, and run away far enough for him not to find us. When Mrs. Munson told us about stranger danger in Health class she told us that if we ever got followed we should just go up to a house with a light on and knock on the door, make it look like you live there.

"But, miss, what if nobody's in?" Kaz asked. "What if someone's like chasing you with a weapon?"

"Yeah!" Angela said. "Or like what if you knock on the door of a pedophile or something?"

Mrs. Munson looked grim for a moment and then said, "Well

you'd be very unlucky, wouldn't you? You'd know your number was up."

She showed us a public information film about a girl who gets in a car with a man who chats her up by the side of the road. And then it doesn't tell you what happens next—the camera work just goes all wobbly and warped and then there's a shot of some roses by the side of the road.

"I don't get it," Kaz said. "Did she get run over or what?" Mrs. Munson glared at Kaz. "It's an *artistic* interpretation, Karen, of what *might* happen if you get into a car with a strange man."

"What might happen?"

Mrs. Munson started to go red. "*Things*." And then she made us look at our fact sheets in silence for the ten minutes before the bell, and nowhere on the bits of paper that she gave us did it say what those "things" were.

"Natasha." I nudge her with my elbow. "*Natasha*."

"Ngh?"

"We've got to *think*."

"What?"

"We need a plan."

"Oh." She sounds sleepy, bored, even. I don't understand why she's just accepting this. It doesn't make sense.

"Well, you must have run away from him for a *reason*. I mean, this isn't exactly what I'd call traveling in *style*."

And then she says something really odd. "Don't think about me. Pretend I'm not here."

That makes me want to cry. Not because of her, but because it makes me even more frightened. I can't understand why she's not being nice to me; we're in this together now, and why doesn't she even want to try to run away?

"You can't just give in," I say to her. "There's two of us now,

61

if we both try together we could get away. I know we could. We just need a *plan*."

She laughs. "Ha! I had a plan once. And now I am here. Plans are no good." And she mutters to herself in a language I can't make out.

Every time I think we're stopping, the car speeds up again. Outside there's a different kind of traffic noise, the heavy vibration of bigger engines: trucks. We're going much faster, the wind whistles through the gaps in the chassis and the car whines.

"Highway now," Natasha says. "Best to sleep."

After a while it gets so hot I can't help closing my eyes. I can see manic pulses of red and yellow behind my lids. I read somewhere that when you fall asleep your eyes roll up in their sockets. Maybe I'm asleep and it's my brain that I'm looking at: flashes of color and light, the pattern of my fear.

8

Hope

"Wake up!"

The water hits my face with a slap. He's got the trunk open halfway and he's splashing us through the gap with water from an Evian bottle.

"Get up!"

Natasha wriggles next to me and groans. She shouts and the man shouts back, but I don't understand what they're saying. "Fucking pig," she mutters under her breath.

When I start to scream, he jabs something at us, at first I think it's a pen or a stick, but then I see the blade. "Shut up! I will stab at you silly bitches."

I want to laugh at his accent and his bad English and his silly Swiss Army knife. Everything is like totally surreal.

"Don't be stupid." I stare at him hard, even though I'm trembling.

Then Natasha starts shouting again and I try to figure out what they're saying, but it's in a language I don't know. Russian, I'm sure of it.

He opens the trunk all the way, grabs me by the wrist and pulls so I have to stand up and jump out. I get really scared again then, when I see where we are. In the distance I can see a road through a chain-link fence, a car sweeping past. In front of us are low, corrugated factory buildings. It's damp and gray, clouds hanging low in the sky. I can't tell if it's early morning or evening. There are no streets, no houses, no friendly lights on in the porches.

He looks at me and laughs. Natasha swears at him as she clambers out.

"*Prick.*"

"*Past'zabej, padla jebanaja!*" He shouts at her. "*Blyadina!*" And he waves the knife in her face.

She flinches when he says this and looks at the floor.

"Where are we? Are we in England?" I look for familiar signs, clues, anything.

"Come on." He shoves me in the back and stabs the air in the direction of the factory. Tox is spray painted on the walls, the doors. I must remember this, for when I talk to the police. For a moment it's like I can see my life as a storyline on TV, on *CSI*, with all the detectives having cool FX flashbacks and Jorja Fox pouting and frowning and looking pensive over partial fingerprints. But all that stuff usually happens *after* the event . . . when they've found a dead body buried in a shallow grave.

A train thunders past close by, making the ground shudder. Natasha slouches and scratches her face. I can't believe she's not even that nervous or scared. She calls him Durak over and over. I wonder if that's his name, though from the way she's saying it, spitting the word out of her mouth like it has a nasty taste, I don't think so.

Inside is gloomy and dark, piles of boxes line the walls, and it smells of damp and dust and cardboard slowly going soft.

Water drips through the holes in the roof, and there's stuff spilling out of the boxes on to the floor. Happy Millennium 2000! it says on a faded plastic banner. I look in one box that is full of Muppets, green Kermit legs dangling over the side. Another box is full of *Playboy* calendars from 2003. A landslide of naked Katie Prices. It says *Mr V. C. Rocci Trading Company* on one of the delivery notes, then, London E8.

"We're in London!"

Natasha doesn't even blink. "Okay." She shrugs.

Durak fumbles around for the lights until one bare strip light flickers and holds. I can see now that we are at the back of the warehouse. In front of us, boxes going forward all the way to the far end. Everything you could ever want—TVs, washing machines, DVD players, dishwashers, PCs.

Another train goes past, this time even louder, a screeching noise echoes around inside the building. He points with a penknife to the floor. "Sit!"

When he gets close I can smell his breath, see the blunt stubbly hairs on his chin.

It makes me think of how Kaz got really bad skin after making out with Jason, the manager of the Liquid Bar, when he hadn't shaved. Red, blotchy, stubble rash where his hairs had scratched her face. I was staying at her place supposedly doing homework and she moaned about it all the way back in the taxi—that she looked like a freak and thank God it was Friday night, so she could stay home all weekend with face masks on. Next time we went to Liquid she ignored him and we all got barred for being underage. Didn't matter anyway, because they still let us in at the Planet.

But I don't know why I'm thinking about them now, they seem so small and far away from here it terrifies me.

Natasha shouts at Durak in Russian again. He's tying her hands together behind her back with duct tape and she's wriggling and spitting at him. It's my turn next. He ties it hard, the adhesive pinching the skin on my wrists.

"Ow!"

Then he takes Natasha's bag and empties it all over the floor.

My clothes, my underwear and my secret savings purse that I kept hidden in the wardrobe all drop out.

"You took my money," I say flatly, too shocked to be upset.

She won't look at me. "I will give back."

"I would have lent you stuff if you'd asked."

Some twenty-pound notes flutter out of the bag, Durak picks them up and stuffs them in his pocket. Then he goes up to Natasha and slaps her and shouts at her again in Russian. When she shouts back he gets really angry. Finally he tapes her mouth with the duct tape.

I don't say anything. I don't want him to do that to me. He kicks all the clothes in the bag into a dusty corner—my Paul Frank T-shirt, my Gap jeans—and paces up and down, not even looking at us.

My mind hums with panicked questions. Why am I here? What are they going to do to me? Will it hurt? How can I escape? Like I can't shut it off. More trains scream past.

"You won't get away with this, you know," I say finally, my voice sounding indignant and prim after the loud screeching of the trains. "My father's a businessman. He's got money, he could pay . . ."

"Eh?" He snarls like a cartoon, his lip curling almost up to his nose. "Eh?" He comes closer, his fist clenching.

I don't want to see his teeth or the hairs up his nose or the slick of his hairstyle. I look at the dusty concrete floor. While we wait, he paces around and shouts at Natasha.

I don't know how long we're there before they arrive, an hour maybe. Long enough for my arms to get sore and ticklish and for Durak to get bored and start flicking through a *Playboy* calendar.

The longer we wait the harder it gets to breathe. Surely they will realize they've made a mistake when they see me. I'm English. It's just a mistake. It's Natasha's fault.

There's some shouting and laughing and then four men turn up. They stand around Durak, shake his hand, cuff him on the shoulder. He laughs and tries to look relaxed, but I can see that he's sweating.

Then a fifth man comes in, tall and impassive in a stripy business suit. He's got the kind of shiny orange tan people have in the south of France. He must be the boss. The men all shut up and look at him. He talks fast, pointing at me and Natasha.

Then he comes over to us. He pulls the tape from Natasha's mouth which makes her squeal but she doesn't say anything. He grabs her by the elbow and makes her stand up. He twirls her around, pats her bottom, looks in her eyes, like he's examining her.

Durak pulls some passports out of his pockets and shows them to the boss. He holds them up to the light. Then he turns round and looks at me and asks me something I don't understand. I shrug my shoulders.

"He wants to know, are you Russian or Ukranian?" Natasha hisses in English.

"I'm English! Tell him I'm English! What's going on?"

I'm not sure this makes things better or worse. The men start shouting at Natasha and at Durak and then one of them gets a gun out of his pocket and starts waving it about. For a second I can't believe it's real, but then I look at Natasha—she's got her eyes closed and she's mumbling like she's praying. I can't stop my body from trembling. Durak puts his hands over his head like that's going to protect him. He keeps pointing at Natasha and shouting.

Suddenly, without warning, the boss shoots Durak in the head, right through the hand he is holding up. His legs crumple underneath him, and he falls over, like someone's cut his strings. Baf! Gone. Just like that.

Natasha shrieks and starts to cry. I scream and then retch,

but there's nothing in my stomach. I wonder if it hurts to die like that.

"Where's Marie?"

My cheek stings from the slap. I didn't even see him coming at me.

"Eh?"

Then he does the same to Natasha.

"I ordered two girls! Two classy girls is what I paid for! And now I have two worthless bitches!" His voice echoes around the warehouse. "How old are you?" He looks at me.

"Fif—fifteen." I can hardly get the words out.

He taps his thigh with his gun like he's trying to weigh up a decision.

"My—my parents will be looking for me. I don't know what all this is about. I—"

Slowly he lifts the gun and points it at me. I close my eyes. It's really weird, but I think if I'm going to die, if he's going to shoot me, then I don't want his face to be the last thing I see. Instead, Mum's face appears in my head and that makes me start to cry. I hope it won't hurt.

I hold my breath until I start to feel dizzy, white stars blink and explode behind my eyes. I'm really afraid I'm going to pee. Natasha whimpers beside me. Then there's a loud shot, a fizz in the air above my head. I flinch, but I'm not hit. I open my eyes a little bit, just to check, and I wonder for a second if I *have* died. The air is full of pastel confetti—horseshoes, wedding bells, hearts—snowing down around me. I look up and get a face full of dust and shot-up bits of box.

He laughs, but it sounds more like screaming, kind of tense and hysterical. "An English girl! No one brings me English any more, not with so many other varieties to choose from."

He shows me the photo page of a British passport: Marie Evans, b. Luton 1990. The girl in the photo is a dirty blonde with sharp cheekbones and dark eyebrows; she doesn't look very English and she definitely doesn't look like me. My face is rounder, my hair a mousier brown.

"So, what I want to know is why *you* are here and not *her*?"

"*He* took me." I nod at Durak's body. His dead face is stuck at a leery angle; lips drooping, eyes half closed. "I want to go *home*. Look, I won't say anything if you let me go. I promise I won't tell anyone. It's just all a big mistake, right?"

He looks at me, making his eyes big, and smiles, showing lots of gold teeth. "Right. With girls it's always a big mistake. Always so much *trouble*."

He flips open a mobile and barks into it.

"Did you know about this? Where's Marie?" I hiss at Natasha. She shuffles away from me on the floor. "You *knew* he would come and find you?" I nod at Durak's body. There's a thick pool of blood seeping into the concrete. "And on the boat, you knew he needed another girl?" I can't believe it, she set me up.

"No! It's not like that!" she mumbles. "I'm sorry."

"You *wanted* Durak to take me?" If I could move my arms right now I'd stand up and grab that gun and shoot her myself. But suddenly she's laughing at me.

"What did you call him?"

"Durak."

She giggles again. "That's not his name."

"Well I only said it because you did."

"Do you know what it means?"

"*No.*"

"Asshole! You think his name is asshole! Ha ha ha!"

"I don't know why you're laughing, he's dead now."

And I realize that she isn't really laughing at all, her body is trembling, her teeth gritted, she's almost crying. "His name was Zergei. He came from Chechnya."

"Why did he bring me here?"

"Because if he didn't"—she nods at the man barking into the phone—"he would hunt him down and kill him."

"Is he *buying* us?"

"Yes." Natasha bites her lip. "Although, maybe now he's *stealing* us."

The boss man snaps his phone closed and strides over to us. "You will shut up!" He raises his arm and I flinch, but he doesn't hit me. Then he shouts something and one of his men comes over and sticks a big piece of silver tape over my mouth. All I can taste is chemicals and glue and I can't breathe at all, my lungs feel like they're going to burst.

"Breathe in your nose," Natasha hisses. "Slowly."

I sniff through my nose and cough and then it gets a bit easier. Natasha wriggles closer to me. "Breathe," she says. "Breathe."

The boss man laughs at us and lights a cigarette. Two of his men lift Zergei's body and take it away. His limp arms drag at an awkward angle along the floor. I don't want to look. I stare at the concrete so hard it's almost like I can see every grain, every particle. This isn't happening to me, I think. This isn't real. And I close my eyes as tightly shut as I can force them. I hope I wake up soon.

9

Oksana

Outside the door the Turkish are talking about the English girl again, although I can't understand everything they're saying because my Turkish is not so good. They talk about how little money they paid for her and if she is really a virgin. One of them laughs and threatens to come and check. And they are confused, because they know now that she isn't really from Italy like the boss man told them, because her English is too good.

She's in the corner, as far away from me as possible.

She's been crying and calling out for her mother since they brought us here. I almost felt bad and put my hand on her shoulder or something, but I can't feel sorry for anyone who still has a mother. They are the lucky ones, only they don't even know it yet.

The boss man shot Zergei. I don't know what to think about this. He went down so quickly. Even though I know bullets kill people dead, I still thought he might get up and fight back.

He was in trouble before he even got here—late, the car scratched and muddy, with only half the order, snivelling that he couldn't do it without backup. That it wasn't his fault. He was just following instructions. He tried to tell them that Hope was a replacement from the Ukraine. But even I can see she looks English. His story didn't make sense. He tried to make out like we were models, the best-quality girls.

71

"I got contacts everywhere," he said.

He should have known better. Boss men don't like people who lie. Who make out like they're tough when really they're jumpy and messed up. It's not good for business. That's how mistakes happen. Mistakes like me and the English girl.

I wish now I had never picked her van. Or I should have got out and run away first chance I got. Now I will never find Adik.

I don't want to work for them anymore, ever. For a moment, back in the English fields, I thought I would never have to. It seemed possible to be free like the birds, flitting around in the crops as the sun came up. Now there is a heavy cloud of feeling somewhere just above my head, threatening to drop down and crush me. I look at the floor and count the threads in the carpet, the balls of dust and hair in the corners, the dirty pink roses in the pattern of the wallpaper.

"Hello, my name is Natasha." Over and over like a tableau at the fair that only moves when you feed it with money. "Hello, my name is Natasha," in twenty-six different languages. I remembered them all one by one when I was in Italy. One by one—*Bonjour! Je m'appelle Natasha; Hallå! Jag heter Natasha; Hallo! Ich bin Natasha*—looking at the horrible wallpaper, the carpet worn shiny by the door, where the customers came in and out. One language for every rose in the room. *Yasas! Me leni Natasha.*

Tommy told me I would make enough money to move me and my family to Moscow one day and live in Rublyovka where all the rich ladies live with many servants, where they dye their poodles to match their outfits. And everyone drives a Mercedes and eats the best caviar and steak and drinks champagne and gold vodka, and there are dishwashers and washing machines and everything you need to be happy and successful in life. He said Europe was better than I could ever imagine, McDonald's on every street—and so *cheap*—Coca-Cola, Burger King, and all the shoes and dresses I could ever want. Better than the pictures in the magazines they started selling in the store. He told me I deserved it because I was pretty, and all pretty girls deserved the good things in life. He said it would be like the life I always dreamed of, but even better, because it would be real.

What a joke.

The English girl is making noises in her sleep, shouting out for Natasha now. She is better to be quiet. She hasn't learned yet, the best way is not to speak, not to complain. Complaining gets you noticed, and getting noticed gets you into trouble.

I sit on her bed, and stroke her hair to quiet her. I don't say anything because it's better not to feel sorry for anyone. If you feel anything for anyone they just get taken away and all the feelings get smashed to pieces until you go cold and numb, like a stone.

The boss has sold us to some Turkish men. I heard him on the phone. He complained about Zergei. Said he'd never trusted him. That he was dealing in third-rate girls and always screwing up. He wanted high-class, he said, for his bar. Not some used up bitches from God knows where. He put tape over Hope's mouth so the Turkish couldn't know that she might be English until it was too late. He got twelve thousand for us, with Zergei's Lexus thrown in.

The Turkish came and got us in a white van and drove us tied up in the back to this place, above a fried chicken restaurant, somewhere not so far away from the warehouse. They put a blanket over me, but I could still see the sign for Dixie Chicken flashing through the material.

I don't know what class of a place this is, but it smells bad. Even in Italy it was better than this. In the corner there is green mold coming through the wallpaper and there are two beds crammed in the room, with only a small space by the door to stand up and get changed.

"Life in London," Tommy said, "is the sweetest." And he kissed his lips like he'd just tasted the best caviar. "In that city, you can have everything you want."

Hope has her eyes open and she's looking at me.

"Are they going to kill me?"

She asks too many questions. She's so stupid and scared it's a pain. I don't want to be nice to her anymore. What is the point? Maybe if I had followed Zergei's plan on the ferry and not been sorry for her because she looked lonely and lost, I would be out of here by now. Instead, I'm right back where I started.

"No," I say. "They only kill you if you run away."

"Really?!" She looks even more scared now.

I pick at the threads in the mattress. "If they kill me I will be saying, 'Yes! Please!' Although really I am frightened to die. If I was brave like Marie I would have thrown myself in the canal when I had the chance."

"You're crazy." She sits up and pulls her knees to her chest. "You're a weirdo!" And she starts shouting for help again, but there's no one who can help us here. And after a while she stops and folds herself up into a ball on the bed, her arms over her face.

Once upon a time, when I was younger, I thought it was possible to get rescued. I thought someone would come like a prince in the old stories. Riding into town on his best horse, to pick me up and sweep me away through the forest to somewhere good, somewhere exciting, like America where Britney Spears lives. I used to long for it every night so hard that when Tommy turned up, I wasn't surprised. After all, I'd wished for him.

I stand up and wash my face in the little sink in the corner. The water smells different from the water in Italy, or the water you could pull from the well in our dacha—clean, earthy water that smelled of leaves and rain and moss and growing, living things. In Italy, one of the girls got a rash on her face that she said was from the water. Her face went scaly and dry like a lizard. One night soon after, she disappeared. Never came back to our room after her shift. When one of the girls asked Antonio where she was, he laughed and said that he got rid of her because she was scaring off the customers.

To get to the window I have to climb over both mattresses. I can't see through it because the glass is frosted with a pattern of leaves and ferns. I can hear traffic outside, but I can't tell where it is.

"Can you see anything?" Hope's kneeling on the bed beside me.

"No."

"D'you think it's a long way down?"

"Maybe."

She pushes me out of the way and pulls her arm back.

"Wait!" She should wrap her hand in something first. When Adik and the boys went stealing they wrapped their fists in rags, and even then Mikki got cuts up his arm.

She brings her fist down into the glass, but it doesn't break and she falls back on the bed holding her hand. "Ow."

Then there's noise outside, the lock turns with a heavy click. I move away from the window, and Hope lies down, covering herself with a blanket.

"Hello, girls." He smells of cheap cologne and hair wax, of garlic and sweaty skin. He's wearing a leather jacket that

75

doesn't hide his belly—a mound that shifts around above his pants like it lives without him. I don't want to look.

"Food," he says, throwing a McDonald's bag on the bed.

When they opened a McDonald's in the town everyone wanted to go. Adik said that's where you could see the best girls and hear the newest music. But it cost more money than we could think of for a cheeseburger and fries—the same as for a whole month of working in the fields digging potatoes. We went there once, just to see, and hung around outside in the cold, looking through the windows at the people. Dina, the mayor's daughter, was there, with her friend Rita and her boyfriend Oleg, who was wearing a baseball cap backward and an REM T-shirt. They were all laughing like they were in a rock video.

"Do you think they're happy?" Adik asked.

Mikki pushed him over in the snow. "Of course they're happy, stupid. That's why they're called Happy Meals."

Adik scrambled to his feet. "I'm going in."

Once inside, next to the bright lights and fat plastic his saggy gray sweatpants and pale skin looked poor and shabby. Rita and Oleg turned around and pointed and started laughing again. I backed away from the window and hid in the shadows, in case they saw me, in my dirty blue coat and eighties jeans, and thought that I was with him.

But then he came running out at top speed, the fat security man lumbering and shouting after him.

"Run!" he yelled, and we ran like we were competing in the Olympics, the cold air burning our lungs. So fast I could hear the air whistling past my ears. Adik seemed to know by instinct which way to go, weaving through alleyways, turning left then right until in the end we hid in an underpass, just outside town, hot and out of breath and laughing.

"Look!" He unzipped his coat and out tumbled a McDonald's

bag full of fries and burgers—and from his pockets handfuls of sugar packets and these little cups of fake cream. "Happy Meal!" and he laughed like he had just heard the best joke.

It tasted good, even though the fries were cold and the burgers got squashed. Mikki drooped a fry across his lip like a mustache and strode around doing stupid walks that made us laugh so hard we were crying. Then Adik gave us the packets of sugar which we put on our tongues in little pyramids of white crystal.

"Let's run!" Adik bounced up and down on his toes.

"You crazy?"

"Of course!" And he just started running. "We can catch the bus if we hurry."

"But the bus stop's miles away!" Mikki puffed after us.

"No, it's not, and it's all downhill." Adik was already ahead, his shaved head bobbing, only just visible in the darkness. Eventually the town gave way to the fields and then, beyond that, the forest and the long road home.

Sometimes I wonder if I had wings. I felt like I was flying: arms and legs everywhere, mad fast, faster than I ever thought I could run, down the side of the road, stumbling into Adik, laughing, gasping for breath, splashed by puddles, skidding through mud, like I'd never had so much energy. Even Mikki, who was fat like a dumpling, kept up with us, till we came to the last slope, up toward the bus stop, when he dropped back and eventually stopped, and walked the rest of the way toward us, grunting as he tried to catch his breath.

When the bus finally arrived we were cold and squelchy and heavy. Adik got quiet and sat behind me, his arms folded across his chest, staring straight ahead, hard. Mikki fiddled with his coat and then fell asleep. I stayed awake and watched the fields disappear into forest as we bounced and lurched home.

"This is shit," Adik said finally.

I didn't say anything, because Adik's mother left him with the Volkov family when he was a baby, and although he said she paid them to look after him, they treated him badly and made him sleep in the shed with the chickens, and I thought if anyone had it shittier than me, he did.

"How come I got born in this dump? How come when it was my turn to be born I was born *here*? It's not *fair*."

He punched the back of the seat.

"Adik—"

He leaned over and put his face next to mine. "No, Oksana, why do I live in this place? And Americans live in big houses with TVs and a movie room and cars and girls? Because it was my bad luck to be born at the moment I was. If my mother could have waited just a few more seconds I might have been born to someone else in America or something."

He told me once that he thought all the souls in the world lined up in heaven before they were born, and it was just luck which body you ended up with when you got to the front of the line.

"But maybe you would line up for ages and still be poor in America," I pointed out. "And anyway, how do you know? I can't remember before I was born."

He sucked his teeth and his eyes shone with frustration. "Better to be poor in America than *here*. At least in America I can have rich dreams."

Cheeseburger and fries. Hope won't eat any. She lay in bed with her eyes closed the whole time he was in the room. He didn't do anything, or even seem especially frightening. He just gave us the food and looked at the floor and coughed a few times and then left.

"It's not that old," I say, offering her some. "Eat."

She wrinkles her nose. "Makes me want to puke. That stuff's *so* bad for you."

"You don't eat McDonald's?"

She makes a face. "Eugh. You joking? Gives you a heart attack."

This makes me angry then—she's all Missy Missy like she's better than me. I throw a cheeseburger at her. "You are lucky to eat!"

She sighs and turns over. "The police will be looking for me you know."

The light starts to fade outside the window and the room becomes gloomy. I'm dozing, listening to the noise of the traffic, *English* traffic. My mother always said I would travel. When she ran her finger along the lines of my hand, she said I'd go far and see many things in my life. I don't know how she could tell.

She thought I was going to be clever and brave and strong.

After she died I used to be able to hear her voice in my head, clear, like she was standing in the same room. Now I can hardly remember the way she used to look, even though I see her in my dreams. I remember her outline, curly, frizzy hair, but it all got confused and frightening. If only I'd been better, if only I'd tried harder to be strong, if only I'd said no.

10

Oksana

The first thing that happened after she died was Viktor.

Father brought him into the apartment wrapped up in her coat. The blue padded one she wore to the hospital. He put him on the table and told me he needed feeding.

"I don't know how to do it," he said.

I didn't know what to do either. I was only eight years old.

Then the baby coughed and made a little mewing sound, like a kitten. I tried to think what Mother would do. I warmed some milk in a pan and picked Viktor out of the coat and held him on my hip. He was so light and tiny, his face scrunched up and wrinkled like an old man. I fed him from a teaspoon like the kitten we had to feed after Mitzi rejected it. I didn't understand how Mitzi, who was a beautiful, friendly, furry cat, could ignore one of her own kittens. She cuffed it with her paw when it tried to get near her, even hissed and bared her teeth at it.

"Why is Mitzi so cruel?" I asked mother.

"Because she only has enough milk for five kittens and this one is weak and sick and might die." She saw my face and chucked me under the chin. "Don't worry. We'll take care of it."

But it died a week later. Even though I'd been feeding it and had kept it wrapped warm in an old sweater.

"It wasn't meant to live," she said, although that wasn't

80

enough to stop me crying. "In life, everything has a time and a place. We can't change it."

I looked at Victor and felt a weight of fear. He was so little and helpless.

I promised her at the funeral, in front of God and the priest and her coffin, that I'd look after him. I stood up straight, tried to pull a face that said I knew what I was doing when I held Viktor to my shoulder.

I trembled inside to see her face, pale and still, her eyes closed. I wanted the priests to stop with the incense and chanting, and the family to stop laying flowers at her feet. I wanted to run to her and shake her and make her wake up. I wanted to tell her that I loved her.

I watched people filing past her coffin, tipping their hats, the family kissing her forehead. My father, in his only suit, which was too small for him around the waist, bent down and kissed her on both cheeks. Viktor gurgled in my ear and I cuddled him closer so I could feel his breath on my cheek. I don't remember people's faces. When I think about the funeral it was like I was in the middle of a dark sea at night, and all around me the water was moving with the noise of moaning and chanting and I was there clutching on to this little bundle that was Viktor, knowing that if I let go, I'd drown.

On the way out I tipped the priest with Father's money and I smiled at people when they told me they were sorry. I took Father's hand. I didn't cry.

Afterward the neighbors came to our apartment with bottles of vodka. Nosy Mrs. Borodovna and her husband from downstairs, she'd even bothered to put on lipstick and her best shawl. Mila Voldimerov, my teacher from school, and her brothers, and Mom's sister, Svetlana, who was married to Yaris, a banker from Moscow. There were so many people that some of them had to stand in the corridor.

They drank toasts to Mother while I sat on the end of the sofa, still clutching Viktor, even though my arms were starting to ache. They talked about what Father was going to do, now he had two children to feed and no wife to look after them.

"I can't take them," said Tetya Svetlana, tossing her glossy hair and sniffing. She never understood why Mother married my father. "The Droski's are all coach drivers. I don't know why you said yes to him," she sneered last time she came to visit. "You should have waited like your sister for the right opportunity to come along."

Mother disapproved of Svetlana because she put her picture on the Internet and advertised for a husband in America. "Just because she has read the English-Russian phrasebook of love doesn't mean she will be happy," Mother said disapprovingly. Then last year Svetlana met Yaris on a chat forum. He had a big apartment in Moscow and three children and a plenty-of-money job.

"I think Baba Droski should move in with you, just for the time being," said Tetya Svetlana.

"Move in? Where?" Father thumped the table. "You see yourself there is no room. I'm not sharing a bed with my own mother!"

Our apartment only had three rooms. One for me, well, me and Viktor now, one for Mother and Father, and the kitchen with the sofa and the wobbly yellow table.

Tetya Svetlana looked around the apartment with her nose in the air. "Nonsense! You can fit an extra bed in there," she said, waving her hand vaguely toward my room.

"No!" I stood up, Viktor clamped to my shoulder. "I'll look after him!"

As I struggled forward I knocked into the table, pushing it

off the copy of Lenin's speeches that had been holding it up. Svetlana and Yaris took a jump back as the bottle of vodka and all the glasses tumbled to the floor and smashed into brittle pieces.

"Now look what you made her do! Interfering old bird!" Father stood up, suddenly filling the kitchen. "You never did anything for Polina when she was alive! Now you turn up in furs in the hot weather, smelling like expensive stores, and think you are better than us! You want to come here and peck around where you are not wanted!"

Tetya Svetlana gave him a dirty look. "Well you can forget about sending Oksana to us for vacations!"

"Take it easy, eh? Lana is only trying to help." Yaris put his hand on Father's shoulder, but he shoved him away.

"Get off! Leave me alone! Go on, get off! All of you! Go away!" He shouted so loud his face went red then purple. He looked like he was going to explode. Viktor started to cry and people muttered and grumbled as they shuffled away.

Mrs. Borodovna from downstairs grabbed my hand and pulled me into the corridor. She had survived two wars and several famines and had skin so wrinkly she looked like a raisin. Mother called her "the shriveled-up-potato woman." She was mean and angry and poked me hard with her bony fingers if I made too much noise outside her apartment.

"For the baby," she said, handing me a box of powdered baby milk. She put her hand on my head and looked sad for a moment. "Your mother was a good woman," she added, before her face closed over and took on its usual sour frown.

After everyone had left, Father kicked the table until it was too broken ever to be fixed.

"Stupid piece of shit!" he shouted, glass crunching under his shoes. When I cleaned up the mess later, spikes of glass were stuck in the floor so deep I had to dig them out with a knife.

11

Oksana

Father used to say that you didn't need money to be happy, "All the things you need in life are free." He meant me and Mother, all together as a family. Like the way the Beatles sang "All You Need Is Love." But then his wages didn't come through. Nearly three months with no pay. And it was the middle of January.

I knew Mother would have managed. All the food she had been making and saving, the blackberry jam at the back of the cupboard, the bags of flour she'd hidden under the floorboards in a mouse-proof plastic tub, the meat she was owed from last year. Now that she was gone, I didn't know who to ask or where to go.

"It will get better soon." That's what everybody said. Soon there would be economic progress. Economic progress meant that we would all be rich like the Americans. At least, that's what Father said. But what happened really is that slowly everybody left. Mila Voldimerov went to Moscow, and for two months there was no teacher to replace her, even Mrs. Borodovna went to visit relatives in Kiev and never came back, until it seemed like it was just me and Dad and Viktor and a lot of old people and empty apartments. There was only one overpriced store, but if you complained, the cow behind the counter would only shout at you and tell you to walk to Moscow yourself and buy it cheaper.

The union at the concrete factory gave out food stamps to

workers with children. But they wouldn't accept them at the store. They said they were worth less than money, because the unions took so long to honor them. Sometimes Father swapped them for roubles, though always for much less than they were meant to be worth. But that January even the food stamps had stopped. Now we only had one bag of moldy potatoes and not enough flour left in the tin to make even one little bun.

"There's no food," I said to Father one morning while he made tea with tea bags stolen from the canteen at work. He gave me some, sweetened with two sachets of canteen sugar, before he said anything.

"Maybe Mrs. Borodovna downstairs?"

"She moved away."

"Oh." He blew the steam from the surface of the cup. "Or Mrs. Ivanski across the way. Your mother always got along with them. Maybe ask them if they can spare us a little something."

"I asked them yesterday." In fact, Mrs. Ivanski didn't even answer the door. She shouted at me through it and told me that it was winter and she never opened her door in winter in case of thieves and beggars. "I wish I could help you," she said, "but Mr. Ivanski has taken the key and you can see there is no mailbox."

Father sighed and rubbed his face. "You'll just have to manage. Your mother always managed."

I felt his eyes, sad and angry, like he was trying not to blame me. I sipped the hot sweet tea and struggled to pretend that it was a real breakfast and ignore the band of worry that squeezed my head like a tight hat. Soon Viktor would wake and want to be fed and I didn't know what I was going to give him to eat.

I hadn't been to school since mother died, over six months ago. At first it was kind of fun. Like I had been chosen to live a different life. I had more important things to do looking after Viktor. But now it was winter and the days were short and boring, and I missed it. Adik gave me all the gossip—who was in love with who, who had moved away to live in Moscow and how the mayor had suddenly got very rich and sent his daughter to school in England.

I missed the classes too. I missed learning about history, about the revolutionaries and the czars, about the war with Hitler and all the brave Russian soldiers who gave their lives for our country. I wanted to get better at English too, because Adik said that speaking English meant one day you could go to America, and if you wanted to study at the university you could read law over there, and lawyers made the most money of all. More even than gangsters sometimes.

In the kitchen there was a corner with all Mother's religious pictures. Painted icons of Mary and Jesus and all the saints. She used to kiss them every morning and say a little prayer for God to bless our family. Since she died, Father had been ignoring them, and I suddenly wondered if this was why we had no money.

I touched them with my fingers. There was one of Jesus on a cross floating above the fires of hell with little black demons nipping at his toes.

"What's that?" I asked Mother once.

"Jesus descending into the fiery furnace of hell."

"Oh. Didn't it hurt?" The expression on his face was kind of resigned yet serene.

"Of course."

"Well how come he looks happy then?"

"I don't know, *kroshka*, it was a cheap one; I bought it in the market."

I touched it now, even though the little demons scared me,

and prayed to God for a miracle so I would find food for Viktor today.

But it didn't seem to work. Viktor grizzled at me all morning until I got so fed up with it I took him out. We walked around and around all the apartment blocks and then down the main road toward the store.

Once we were there, the shabby advertisements in the window for cheap yogurt and vodka made us hungry, and before I knew it we were inside, touching the packets of food.

The assistant, in an ugly gray sweatshirt with a yellow logo flashed across the chest, stared at me as I pulled Viktor away from the candies. He couldn't understand why I wouldn't let him open a packet right there in the store.

"I need milk for the baby," I said, grabbing Viktor and holding him under my arm.

"People need many things," said the woman behind the counter, flicking over another page of her magazine. "What am I supposed to do about it?"

"Please," I said, hot with the shame of asking. "I can pay you back."

"They all say that." She looked up and gave me a weak smile. "Sorry."

I thought about stealing then. Just walking out of the store with all the things I needed, but I knew she would call the police because the store took the losses out of her wages. Viktor snuffled and mewed in my arms. He was still too small. His baby bones showed through skin that was slack and wrinkled instead of plump and smooth. One mashed up potato a day isn't enough for a baby.

"*Please.*"

She looked at me then like I was a piece of shit.

"My father works at the concrete factory. Soon he will get paid. I will pay you back."

She snorted. "At the concrete factory? They will never get paid. They will be closing it down soon! Don't you know anything?"

"That's not true!" They couldn't close down the concrete factory. Russia always needed concrete. Father said that. "Every generation they knock the whole country down and start building it again. Concrete is God's gift to the Russian people."

She snorted when I said this. "God's gift?! I can think of better things he could give me. Your father sounds pretty stupid. What d'you think?" She curled her lip at me. "What I don't understand is why people like you have so many babies."

"He's not mine. He's my brother."

She stared at me impassively. "What's the difference?"

"He's my brother," was all I could say. "My brother." I held Viktor up to the counter, so she could see how pale and small he was.

She sucked her teeth. "Well, I suppose I can take vouchers. If you don't have any cash." She made out like she was doing me a big favor.

"We don't have any left." Her face froze over again. "Maybe if I could just take the milk? And then we can pay you back when I get the voucher? My name is Oksana Droski. I live—"

"I can't help you."

She folded her arms across her chest, like that was the end of the conversation.

I stared at her. I couldn't believe she could be so cruel over one lousy pint of milk. I gathered up all the saliva I could suck out of my cheeks and spat it at her. Slimy strings of it landed in her hair. "Bitch," I said, very loudly and deliberately.

I didn't stay around to hear what she said next.

Outside the weather was like hell. The sky already gray, the wind cold enough to slice you into pieces. I pulled Viktor closer to my chest and tried to figure out how to make three potatoes last us until next week. If the bitch was right and the factory was going to close, then what would happen to us? All the way home I worried so my mind was knotty from turning the same problem over and over in my head and all I could smell in my nose was baking bread, tantalizing, making my stomach grumble. If Mother was here I wouldn't even be allowed outside in such weather.

"Hey!"

Adik sat on the floor with his back to our door. His face was blue and purple with cold. He was holding his arms around himself and shivering like a dog.

"Hey! Where have you been? I'm freezing to death out here!" He was trying to be cheerful, but that just made me feel worse. He looked like death. "Can I stay at yours?"

"I don't know what for. We don't have anything."

When Mother was alive she would always find enough for Adik, an extra slice of bread, some leftover *solyanka*—leftovers! My stomach ached. She said we should love Adik because he had even less in life than we did. Now, suddenly, neither of us had anything and I didn't want him hanging around making me feel bad about not being like my mother.

"It's okay. I brought you a present," he said, like he was reading my thoughts. He handed me a plastic bag. He was grinning so it had to be something good. When I looked inside I could have jumped on him and kissed him. Bread, milk, packets of soup, a small wrap of cheese, and, oh miracle! A piece of meat.

"And . . ." He zipped open his thin tracksuit jacket. "Some drink." He flashed a bottle of vodka.

I did not ask him where he got it. Which person who fell asleep on the bus on the way home from work had their shopping stolen from under their feet.

Adik helped me chop up onions and potatoes and I filled the pan with water and powder from the packets of soup. I cut a small corner off the meat and put it in the pot. The rest I wrapped up and saved for later in the plastic flour tub. I thought how surprised Father would be when he came home, the apartment warm with the smell of cooking.

We fed Viktor small chunks of bread soaked in milk while we waited for the stew. He sucked them down so quickly he was sick all over Adik and then he cried so much we couldn't get him to eat anything at all. Adik bounced him on his shoulders, trying to calm him.

"Hold him tight and still and tell him a story." It was a relief to have someone else take him, even if it was only for a few minutes. My arms were long and heavy from carrying him all day.

"Once upon a time there lived a grandmother and grandfather," Adik started, but Viktor just yelled even louder.

"WHO WERE VERY POOR AND HAD NOTHING AT ALL IN THE WHOLE WORLD." Adik yelled the story at Viktor. "THEY GOT POORER AND POORER. SO POOR, THAT EVENTUALLY THERE WAS NOTHING AT ALL LEFT TO EAT IN THE HOUSE. SO THE GRANDFATHER SAID TO THE GRANDMOTHER, 'BAKE ME A BUN, GRANDMOTHER! IF YOU SCRAPE OUT THE FLOUR BIN YOU'LL HAVE ENOUGH FLOUR.'"

Adik paused to wipe snot and tears and vomit from Viktor's face. His crying had stopped just a little bit, now he was sobbing gently.

"So the grandmother scraped out the flour bin, and mixed some dough and made a little round bun. She lit the oven and baked the bun and then put it on the windowsill to cool. But you'll never guess what happened next!"

Viktor gurgled and grabbed Adik's finger with his hand.

Even though I had heard the story a hundred times, Adik still made it sound like a different one every time he told it.

"The little round bun knew it was going to get eaten by the grandmother and grandfather with no teeth and stinky breath, so it jumped right out of the window and away it rolled along the road! On and on it rolled until it met a rabbit coming toward it.

"'Mmmm, a little round bun!' said the rabbit. 'I'm going to eat you up!'

"'Please don't eat me, Rabbit,' said the little round bun. 'I'll sing you a song instead.'

"'A song?' The rabbit twitched his whiskers uncertainly. He wasn't sure that the little round bun with a squeaky voice would sing a very good song. But sing it did.

> *I ran away from Grandpa,*
> *I ran away from Grandma,*
> *And now I'm going to run away from you!*

"And as it sang the little round bun rolled away down the road laughing to itself . . ."

And so the story went on, and I watched Adik, holding Viktor and telling him about the wolf and the bear that were outwitted by the little round bun in exactly the same way as the rabbit. By the time he got to the fox, Viktor was asleep. But Adik didn't stop. His voice just got quieter and quieter. So quiet I had to lean over and put my head right near Adik's face.

"After a while little round bun met a fox coming toward it.

"'Mmmm, delicious, a little round bun,' said the fox. 'I'm going to eat you up.'

"'Please don't eat me, Fox,' said the little round bun. 'I'll sing you a song instead.'

"'A song?' The fox twitched his handsome red face. He

wasn't sure that the little round bun with a squeaky voice would sing a very good song. But sing it did.

> *I ran away from Grandpa,*
> *I ran away from Grandma,*
> *I ran away from Rabbit,*
> *I ran away from Wolf,*
> *I ran away from Bear,*
> *And now I'm going to run away from you!*

"'I'm sorry?' said the fox. 'My hearing is very bad these days. Could you be so kind and come a little closer so I can listen to your marvelous song? Hop on to my tongue so I can hear you better.'

"So little round bun jumped on to the fox's tongue and began to sing.

> *I ran away from Grandpa,*
> *I ran away from Grandma—*

"But before it could go on, the fox opened his mouth and—snap!—the little round bun was gone."

Adik laughed softly. "That's the way of the world, little Viktor. In this life you have to always watch out for the fox."

And then the stew was ready and Adik put Viktor to sleep on the couch and lit a candle and we huddled around the table slurping up the hot food. And even though I was only nine years old I felt like I was about a hundred and three already. But that night, for a short while, the world was normal again: me, Adik, and Viktor, safe and warm, eating our supper. Just like everybody else.

12

Hope

I lie on the bed and scratch at the wallpaper with my fingernails. It comes off in thin, damp strips. I wonder how long it would take to scratch my way out of here.

There's a dim orange light coming through the frosted window, and the occasional blue flash and wail of sirens. The first time I thought it was the police come to rescue me. I waited for the knock and thump of footsteps outside. But nothing happened.

This is all a big mistake. I can't believe they don't know that. I can't see why they want me anyway. Natasha said they were stealing us. Perhaps she meant kidnapping, but this seems like a weird sort of place to hold people. And I don't like the way the men look at me. It's like a bad dream I can't wake up from.

Natasha lies on the bed next to me. She tosses and turns and shouts in her sleep. I want to punch her. It's her fault I'm here. Bitch.

There are muffled noises all around us. Voices in the corridor, footsteps outside our room, traffic thundering on the road. There's still a cold burger on the bed, fat congealing on the wrapper. It makes me feel nauseous. My clothes are sticky and dirty and my head aches.

Then there's a noise, close by, outside the room. Shouting in another language I don't understand. A bright fluorescent light flickers on. The door is unlocked and Natasha wakes up with a start.

"Get in!" a voice growls, and two girls are pushed inside and the door is banged shut again behind them.

Then the light is switched off and they stand in the doorway, blinking. I can't really see them properly, two thin shadows in the darkness.

Natasha says something in Russian, then in another language I don't know.

"She is Lulu and I am Ekaterina," the taller shadow says, in English with a thick accent. "From Sweden."

Natasha snorts and says something that sounds like "Estonia."

Ekaterina shrugs. "You are new?" She looks at me.

"Yes," I say. "I'm here by mistake. You have to tell them it's a mistake."

She sucks her teeth and doesn't say anything. Lulu sits on the end of my bed and sniffs. "*My* bed," she mutters before turning to Ekaterina and talking in a weird language like I'm not even there.

I get up and run to the door and start to bang on it. "Let me out!" I shout so loud it tears at my throat. I kick the door as hard as I can with my foot. The wood gives a little against the lock, the bottom panel moving forward a few centimeters. For a second I think it might be possible to push it out so I can crawl through like it's a cat flap. I kick it again in the corner, but this time someone shouts and then the door opens, nearly hitting me. Fat Burger Man is standing in front of me, squinting and angry like he's just been woken up.

"Shut up!" he shouts. I flinch, not sure what to do. I wonder what would happen if I ran at him, if I could wriggle past. He balls his hand into a fist. "Yes?" he growls. "What you want?"

"I'm sorry," I say, looking at the dirty carpet. "But I have to go *home*. This is just a big misunderstanding. I'm not supposed to be here." It comes out more like a mumble than a demand. I clench my teeth to stop them from chattering.

He stares at me like he doesn't know what I'm talking about. "You shut up or I get boss."

"You can't keep me here!" I'm shouting now but I don't care. "My dad is coming to get me!"

He laughs like I've just told him a joke. "You can *not* go." He leans across the door and grabs me by the wrist. "You stay here."

"Let me go!" He tightens his grip, twisting, so it burns my skin.

Then Natasha's behind me. "Be *quiet*," she hisses in my ear. "*Please*."

There's something about the way she's pleading that scares me. Fat Burger Man is laughing, showing yellow teeth and oily, sloppy lips.

"You listen to your friend," he says, dropping my arm and pushing me backward. As I stumble he slams the door and locks it again.

"You no make trouble," Ekaterina says, climbing on to my bed next to Lulu, taking my space.

Now there's no room for me. "Where am I supposed to sleep?"

She shrugs. "You sleep on floor. This is *our* bed."

Oddly, Lulu puts her hand inside her top, pulls a few notes out of her bra and smoothes them flat against her thigh. She folds the notes into small squares and stuffs them into the edge of the mattress. "You touch, I kill you." She stares at me.

"I don't need your stupid money! I want to go *home*!" I don't understand why they're being so horrible to me.

She sticks her finger up, her nails red and chipped.

"Why you here?" She says this like she's accusing me of something. "You're not one of us."

"I don't know. There's been a mix-up or something. I was with her—" I point at Natasha but she's lying down again, with her back to us, staring at the wallpaper.

"Then they will be looking for you," Lulu says simply. "And that will bring trouble for us. If the police come they will kill you."

"Kill me?!" Fear pulls at my heart muscle. "Why? What have I done?"

She doesn't answer that. "This is *my* bed. You sleep with *her*."

I sit down on the bed next to Natasha. This is like a weird, horrible dream. I don't know what I've done wrong, yet I feel kind of guilty.

Lulu lights a cigarette. The end glows in the darkness and the air fills with thick smoke.

Behind me Natasha sighs and turns over. "Don't pay attention to them," she says quietly. "They're from Estonia. Only crazy people come from Estonia."

"Oh."

She moves back toward the wall a bit, leaving me enough room to lie down. "You can have room here."

"Thank you."

She turns away from me again like she doesn't want to talk.

"Natasha?"

"Mmm?"

"Can I ask you a question?"

"Mmm."

"Why are we here?"

She sighs but doesn't say anything. I don't really want to hear the answer anyway, because I know it will be bad. It's against the law, to buy people and shut them up in dirty rooms, but my mind is so confused. Maybe I did do something, but I can't remember it. Home seems like a whole lifetime away. And in between it's like my head has been full of fuzz and panic. I rub my arms. I'm not cold, but my body is clammy and shivery, like the time I got knocked off my bike by a car speeding down the lane. Mum said I was in shock and made me drink a cup of sweet tea.

The girls mutter and shuffle about on the beds. There's a crackling sound and the flick of a lighter and the room is filled with a sticky, chemical smell, like burning plastic. Natasha sits up and sniffs.

"*Ty shto delaesh?!*"

The girls mumble something but don't turn round. Natasha looks really angry and jumps out of bed.

"Stupid!" she says, standing over them, then she shouts something else in Russian.

I stand up to see over her shoulder. Lulu has got a bit of tinfoil and she's holding a lighter underneath it. I think for a moment that she must be trying to start a fire. But there's some oily stuff on the tinfoil that burns, and as it burns she sucks up the smoke with the tube from an empty pen.

"Why do you do this?" Natasha is really upset. She knocks on Lulu's head with her knuckles. "*Hello?* Anybody home?"

Lulu swipes her away with her hand, clumsy and floppy, and passes the foil to Ekaterina. Then she lies back on the bed and groans. In the flickering glow of the lighter her eyes are white as moons.

Natasha sucks her teeth and sits on the bed next to me. "Stupid," she mutters. "Stupid," she says again, loud enough for them to hear. Lulu sticks a lazy finger in the air at us and her friend blows out a slow breath of smoke, like someone letting air out of a balloon.

"You want some?" Ekaterina asks, holding out the piece of foil to me.

"What is it?"

"They give it to them," Natasha says, pointing at the door. "You don't touch."

Ekaterina shrugs and bends over for another hit. After that she falls asleep, still sitting up, her head bent into her lap, hands clasped together like she's trying really hard to hold on to an invisible piece of rope.

I wait for a while until Natasha is obviously asleep. I need something heavy that will smash the window in one go. I feel around under the bed but there's nothing except dust and greasy carpet. I stand up as silently as I can. I don't want to wake them until I have to. In the corner under the sink there's a garbage bin made out of some kind of rusted metal.

I tip the garbage into the sink and hold the bin in front of me, toward the glass, like a hammer. I take a deep breath. I hope it's not a long way down.

The first time it bounces, but the glass cracks in the corner. Natasha sits up and shouts at me. The other girls don't make a sound. I bring the bin down again quickly, and this time the whole window breaks in crazy jagged lines. I use the bin to shield my arms and knock away the rest of the glass. Chunks of it fall, smashing again as they reach the ground somewhere in the dark tangle of garden underneath. We are three stories up, in the attic, with a steeply sloping roof right in front of me. There's a drainpipe that I might be able to reach if I can get out of the window and find a way to slide down the slates without falling off. At the end of the garden is a thick concrete wall and beyond that a two-way street outlined by rows of orange streetlights. It doesn't look like I expected. I thought I would be able to see the street, houses, even other people. Maybe there's a way to get around the front.

"No!" Natasha grabs my wrist.

I shake her off. "I can't stay here."

The night air is a relief, cold and fresh. I take great lungfuls of it as I bend down and turn around to step out on to the roof. Carefully I try to balance on the tiles, but the grip on my sneakers isn't good enough and my feet start to slip away from me and suddenly I'm sliding toward the edge of the roof with nothing to break my fall. Natasha screams and the fluorescent light flicks on and there are other voices shouting and Fat Burger Man has his head out of the window and he's yelling at me. I press down with my hands, but there's nothing to hold on to. I dig my toes into the plastic guttering as I get to the edge. It creaks, but it doesn't break. It doesn't feel very secure though. I couldn't stand up or hang from it. Beneath, the garden is thick with overgrown brambles and garbage.

It's too far down to jump, and now there's someone crashing around down there anyway, a younger man in a tan jacket and bright white sneakers. He shines a flashlight up at me. At his heels is a snarling, barking dog.

Gingerly, I turn round so I'm sitting, pressing on the drainpipe with my heels. The plastic creaks and I hold my breath to try to make myself lighter.

Natasha leans out of the window.

"My hand! Take my hand!"

Behind her, Fat Burger Man is holding her around the waist. "Quick!"

I don't know what to do. I'm scared of going back and scared of going forward. I can't move.

Natasha's face is going purple with the effort. She's trying to grab me but her fingertips just graze my hair. Fat Burger Man grabs her legs and lowers her farther out of the window.

"Come with me. *Please*." She says, between gasps for breath. "If you don't he will drop me. Then we will both fall and die."

"I don't want to go back in there! Why are they keeping us locked up? What have they bought us for? What are we *doing* here?"

"I tell you! I tell you! But you have to come back inside. *Now*." Fat Burger Man drops her a little lower and she grabs me by the arm. "Hold on."

Slowly, he pulls us both back up. My sneakers slip against the tiles, greasy with moss and algae. When I get to the window another arm reaches under my shoulder to haul me up.

Then there's a lot of shouting and pushing. Fat Burger Man pulls the sheets out from under Lulu and her friend and tips them off the bed like they're laundry. He kicks Lulu in the back while she's still on the floor. Then he turns on me. He shoves his hand against my shoulder and shouts. He waves his fist and pushes me against the bed so I bruise my ankle on the frame. I fight the urge to cry. Then Natasha grabs my hand and says something and he seems to calm down.

"We have to go to another room," she says. "He says you cost him money. He wants to know who is going to pay."

They make us all walk down the corridor to another room, which is almost identical to the last one. Except this time there is no window at all, just a big square of drywall where the window should be. At least there are four beds, but there's mess everywhere. Sheets on the floor, plastic bags, empty McDonald's and KFC bags, cans of beer, and stacks of magazines.

Fat Burger Man shouts something at us and then shuts and locks the door. At least we have a light switch inside.

Natasha starts to pick up the garbage. "He said we have to clean up."

I wrinkle my nose. "For him?!"

"He says he will take the window out of our wages."

"Wages? He's *paying* you to be here?"

Natasha sighs. "No. *We* are paying *him*."

I don't understand. "Paying him? For this?!" I wave my hand at the shabby room.

"Paying him back." She doesn't look up. "It is expensive to come to England. We cannot afford to pay. So he pays and we work and we pay him back."

"Don't lie."

"I don't lie. I am telling the truth. We have to pay them what we earn." Natasha shrugs. "That's business."

I know she's not being completely honest with me, but before I can say anything more I notice there is blood on her leg, and her jeans are ripped where she cut herself pulling me back through the window.

"You're bleeding."

She looks at her thigh and brushes her hand over it. "Only scratches," she says.

I suddenly feel bad for being mean to her. "I'm sorry."

She looks up at me and smiles, just slightly, the corners of her mouth twitching a little. In the dingy light she looks exhausted, the dark hollows under her eyes even more pronounced.

"It's okay," she says. But I know it's not. None of this is okay. We've, *I've*, got to find a way to get out of here.

With the window boarded over, the room is hot and claustrophobic and the strip light makes everything yellow and shiny. The Estonians are huddled under blankets with their eyes shut. I don't understand why they're *paying* to be here. You don't *pay* to be locked in a room and kicked in the head and shouted at.

I wash my face in the sink and look at my reflection in the dusty mirror. I hardly recognize myself. My eyes are puffy and

101

swollen, my skin is gray and blotchy, and my hair is like a thick hedge, all sticking out at funny angles.

I pick up an empty Coke can, some tissues and shove them in Natasha's garbage bag. Next to the bed there's a stack of magazines. I pick one up. *Teen Hotties Special*. I didn't really notice before. They're all dirty magazines.

When I was eleven I went to Kaz's house for tea and she showed me a magazine she found in her brother's room and we giggled at the pictures of the women, posing like dolls, their white breasts shocking and naughty.

This magazine is different. It's just photos of girls in school uniforms, posing like Britney Spears, except every few frames their breasts escape from their too-tight shirts. Further on, there are pictures of men too, and close-up shots of bits of body and people having sex. I feel embarrassed to look, but I can't ignore it.

"What kind of work are you doing"—I hold the magazine so Natasha can see—"*exactly?*"

Natasha stacks the second garbage bag neatly by the door. "What?" she says distractedly, although I know she heard me.

"What do you do? To pay them back?"

She looks at the floor. "In Italy, sometimes dancing," she says. "Here"—she shrugs—"I don't know."

"Is it"—I don't really know how to say it—"like in the magazine?" I flap it at her.

Natasha doesn't answer.

"They want us to have . . . sex with people, don't they?" I feel embarrassed even saying the word. "With men who pay for it. *That's* why we're here."

A sickly rush of realization makes the hairs on my arms stand up. *That's why we're here.* That's how we pay them back. I swallow hard. I've never had sex with anyone before. I don't even know how to do it or if I'll like it. When we did sex in our Health class, Mrs. Munson showed us how to put condoms on a banana.

"What good is that!" Kaz snorted, pinging her condom across the room like a rubber band. "It's not like I'm going to go out with a banana, is it, miss?" And the whole class burst out laughing.

Now I realize why the men have been looking at us like they have: sleazy, sizing us up, and it's not funny at all. The thought of my body being anywhere close to Fat Burger Man makes me feel sick. Like I want to throw up my whole guts. Suddenly, and very urgently, I want to be with Mum. I swallow to stop myself from crying.

"Do you have to—with them?" I point at the door.

Natasha shrugs. "I don't know. Maybe."

"That's disgusting!"

She flinches when I say this and her eyes tighten like she's angry. "Listen, English. You don't know anything about my life! Now I tell you something. My name is not Natasha."

I sniff. "What is it then?"

"Oksana."

"Ox, what?"

"*Oksana*." She stares at me, like she wants me to know something very important. "Oksana Droski. And I'm not supposed to be here either!"

13

Oksana

The girl in the store was right. The factory did get closed down. Men in expensive black suits came from Moscow and said that it belonged to them now because they had a piece of paper stamped by the tax office that said so. The next day all the workers had to line up to apply for their own jobs and some of the older, slower ones never got rehired.

When they hired Father again, they paid him a few roubles right there, when he signed his contract. A goodwill gesture, they said, on account of the fact that the new contract no longer allowed the workers to belong to any unions. And, although the pay was officially less than it was before, at least they *paid*. He pulled out the thin fold of notes to show me.

"See?" he said, kissing the money. "A country that is always building will always need concrete!"

The concrete factory was part of the miracle he said. "The economics miracle that is happening all over the world!" It was like a fever, a spreading fire, soon everyone would have money, a better future, a better chance at life. "It is happening in your lifetime, Oksana. Your children will be blessed."

"Is it a God miracle?" I asked.

He just laughed at me. "No! It is a President miracle!"

"Then it's an *illusion*," I said to him with certainty.

"What?" He stared at me for a moment.

"Human magic is an illusion. That's what Mother said."

He looked like he might be angry with me. His mouth went thin and hard. But when he spoke his voice was thick and croaky.

"Well she's not here to argue anymore is she?" he said. And for a moment I thought he was saying that he was pleased she was dead, except there was one thin tear streaking his cheek, a shiny stripe through the dirt on his face.

The moment Viktor's arms were long enough, he locked them around my neck and set them there, like a lump of concrete. In the morning, he would shout in my ear until I woke up and fed him. Some days he would pretend to be a dog all day and want to lick his water from a bowl on the floor. He whined and pinched and cried so that I started to hate him. And I wished a few thousand times a day that Mother would just walk in through the door and take him away from me.

Even though Father was earning money again it wasn't enough to make us rich. By the time we'd paid for rent and bills there was hardly enough left over for food and clothes. Father said it would get better in a few months when the factory was on its feet again, but as far as I could tell things were just as bad as they were before. How was he supposed to work ten hours a day when he couldn't even feed himself properly? And now that there was no union, there weren't even any food stamps or joints of meat from the collective farm or complimentary canteen sugar.

In about a year Viktor would be old enough to go to school, and then I could go back too. But I would be fourteen by then, and so far behind the others that I'd have to start again, with all the eleven-year-olds.

Adik tried to help in the beginning. He brought me his school books and let me do his homework for him, and played with Viktor and took him out for walks. But then he stopped going so much to school and started hanging out with Mikki and Kolya and Dimitri, and they called each other *Brat* and listened to gangster rap on tapes that Kolya made from recording the radio on an old Dictaphone. They hung around outside the store, protecting the neighborhood and harassing anyone they didn't like.

They called me *Sestra* and let me hang out with them and bring Viktor too. All that summer when I was thirteen we sat around on crates under the tattered green awning that leaked when it rained. Sometimes Mikki and Adik would turn up with "presents": a CD player, a bottle of vodka, a battered old Game Boy that only worked if you held the batteries in while you were playing it, a pair of Levi's that didn't fit anyone.

We were *klevo, kruto*, we were cool—at least that's what Adik said. "Like a family." It was better than being at home all day listening to Viktor whining, but sometimes sitting there, getting ridges in my butt from the hard plastic of the crates, it seemed pointless. I should have been in school, Viktor should have been at home . . . my mother should have still been alive.

He was outside the shop showing off his cell phone to Adik and Mikki and Kolya the first time I met him. They were crowding around him, their pants too small, their mouths too slack. I nearly turned back to go home when I saw him in his shiny suit, with his Ray-Ban sunglasses and the new Audi that he said he'd driven here all the way from Germany.

I didn't want him to see me. My hair was tied up with a strip of cloth that I'd torn out of an old cushion cover and there were holes in my sneakers, and with Viktor's sweaty hand clutching mine, he would think, like most people, that Viktor was my son, and then he'd give me disbelieving looks when I tried to explain.

But Adik waved me over, and Mikki called my name, and there was nowhere to hide or pretend like I hadn't seen them.

"Hey, Oksana! Guess what!" Adik ran some of the way to meet me. "I've got a job!" His face was red and flushed. "Look!" He pulled a note out of his sleeve. A dollar bill. "He gave me this."

I slowed down. No one around here gave away money for free. And how come Adik was so special? He didn't even know how to write his own name. "What for?"

He wouldn't look at me. "Business," he said.

"What kind of business?"

He shrugged. "Tommy's business."

"Tommy?!" I snorted. "Who has a real name like that?" And then an ache of jealousy. How come Adik got to have his dreams come true and not me?

"Who's this?" Tommy asked as we got closer, nodding his head at me. His hair was dark black and cut into a fin at the top. He looked tanned and clean, handsome, and he smelled of expensive cologne like a rock star or a model, not like a Russian.

"Oksana," Adik said, "and her brother, Viktor."

He let out a low whistle and closed the car door. "Hey, princess." And he gave a ridiculous bow like I was some kind of queen. The boys laughed and whooped. I didn't know what to do, stuck somewhere between being flattered and feeling annoyed.

He said he was from around here, and he couldn't understand why no one remembered him.

He said he was working for a big company now and they were doing some speculating in the area. "We value stuff. Decide if something's worth buying."

"What kind of stuff?"

"Oh, just local businesses, stuff like that." He lit a cigarette and kicked at a scruff of brown grass that was growing out of a crack in the curb like it was a football. He didn't seem very good at standing still. "You got a boyfriend yet, princess?"

"*No.*" That was the kind of question Tetya Svetlana always asked when she called from Moscow at Christmas. And then she'd screech with laughter like the idea of me having a boyfriend was some big joke.

"So you hang around with these guys all day? You don't go to school?" He waved a hand at the boys, who were sitting in his car listening to Eminem on the stereo.

"I have to take care of him." I pointed at Viktor who was busy throwing sticks down the drain.

"Ah." He raised his eyebrows like he was disappointed. And for one second I wanted to pick up Viktor and stuff him down the drain too. It wasn't Viktor's fault. I *knew* it wasn't Viktor's fault. But it wasn't *fair.*

Then he got a call on his cell phone and he kicked the boys out of his car, put his sunglasses back on and was gone with a screech of tires and a cloud of gritty dust.

Adik couldn't stop talking about him. "Did you see those sunglasses?" "What about that car?" "He's been to America! London! Berlin! Paris!"

Mikki dragged his toe in a circle. "I don't know, man. What's he doing around here?"

"Like he said. He's come to put some luck back into his old town. That's what *I'm* going to do. One day when I've got loads of money."

"Hey, man! What about us?" Mikki said. "I thought we were coming too!"

"Yeah," I said. "I'm not staying here!" I was offended by the idea that he thought he could go just like that, leaving me behind. "I want a job too."

"Okay, okay. I'll ask him next time I see him."

"I bet we don't see him again," Dimitri, who had been watching us from a distance, said. "I bet he's ex-police or a spy. What does he want with a rat like you?" He came up to Adik, suddenly taller, bigger, better fed.

"You calling me a rat?"

"Yes. And you stink like the chicken shed you sleep in. This isn't a real gang with you in it. You're embarrassing, you're not a brother."

And then they started fighting. I can't even think who threw the first punch it was all so quick. Suddenly Adik was on the floor with Mikki and Dimitri kicking him and Kolya holding him down.

Viktor started yelling and I shouted at them to stop, but it was useless. By the time we got Adik back to the apartment he'd split his lip and gotten two black eyes.

"I tell you, Oksana," he said, struggling to talk, "Tommy will save us. I promise you. I'm going to go to Paris and London and New York and Los Angeles. I'm going to make millions of billions of money."

"And what about me?" Although I didn't believe him for one minute, I still felt a stab of jealousy that he could have such big dreams when he knew I was stuck with Father and Viktor.

"Then I'll come back and marry you!" he said, like this was obvious all along.

"Marry me? Who said I wanted to marry you?" I teased him, though secretly I was pleased.

"When I have all the things, the jewelry and clothes and cars, you won't be able to say no."

I thought about this for a minute. "Can we have a big house?"

"Of course."

"Big enough for Father and Viktor?"

"We can buy them their own houses!"

"Okay," I said. "I'll marry you."

Adik grinned and then winced because it hurt his face. "Can I have a kiss then?"

"A kiss?" I was thirteen and I'd never kissed anyone who wasn't family before.

"Yes, we have to kiss if we're going to get married." He brought his face close to mine, his skin was hot and sore and his lips were cracked and dry and flecked with blood.

I turned my face so he pecked me on the cheek. His lips felt rough and papery but they gave me a ticklish feeling all over my cheek.

"Aw, Oksana," he said, trying to kiss me again.

"Get off!" I giggled, and brushed him away. "You can have a real kiss when you come back with all your money."

"But that might be years away! Can't I have just a little one? Just for now?"

I looked at him. His eye was swelling up so it was nearly closed over. He wasn't about to go anywhere and make lots of money. He was just Adik with a broken face, still thin and scruffy.

"Okay," I said, puckering my lips.

14

Oksana

The Estonians are paranoid. I heard the girls bitching about me in the lounge where they make us wait for the clients, now I have started work for the Turkish too. I know how it is to be them. When new girls come there is always trouble. But they are also very stupid. I figured out in Italy that it doesn't mean, just because the boss squeezes you around the waist in front of the customers, or buys you a drink, that he *likes* you. Because there are always new girls coming along, snapping at your feet; prettier, younger girls who make more money.

They think Hope is here for the Internet. I don't know what this means exactly, but I heard of some places that do live shows that people pay to see online. In Italy, Antonio had a small Web site with pictures of models on it that were supposed to be like us. He only kept six girls at a time, because he said he was offering his clients perfection and it was amazing how quickly ripe fruit went bad in the heat.

"Think about Inter Milan or Juventus," he said one evening when it was the World Cup Final. He would show it on the screens at the bar instead of porn. "Once the players get old and tired their price goes down. So it is with girls."

I never listened to him when he was talking. He liked to talk too much. He wanted to believe that we didn't mind what we were doing—"In Italy we pray to women like you. Have

111

you never heard of Mary Magdalene? For Italians you are a goddess."

After all, it wasn't *his* fault that in the big wheel of the world he was the boss and we were girls. It could so easily be the other way around! He was so full of excuses, even more so than Zergei, to whom he sold me eventually. "I'm not a bad man. I just got born on the wrong side of the bed. Bad things followed my name. So in the end I think, 'What the hell?' and I stop trying to resist."

When there is no money, first of all you look around to see what there is that you can sell. Chairs you can chop up for firewood, bowls or plates, saucepans or knives, a summer dress, sunflower seeds stolen from the fields. But that only buys bits —a bag of flour, maybe bread, sometimes meat, most likely only a little milk—and when that's gone you start to get desperate. You scratch around in your head and try to figure out what else there is in the house that might be worth money. But no one wants a dirty mattress or a broken radio. You need food, soap, new pants to replace the ones that you have grown too tall for, shoes for the winter; you'd like a new stove to replace the one that short-circuits every time you use the oven, some real washing powder to make your clothes smell clean, enough credit to have the heat on in the cold weather.

You get so flat and bored and desperate that you could crush yourself and squeeze out the juice and sell it to the first thirsty person that walks past with money in their pocket. You could grind your bones into flour for pancakes, braid your hair into fisherman's rope, squeeze out your eyes and sell them to a blind man, anything; anything seems better than just sitting, your belly sore with hunger, waiting for something to happen.

But now I wish with all my heart to be back there. I wouldn't mind the cold, Viktor's clingy whining, Adik fidgeting at the sound of every distant engine. That would be like heaven compared to this. Here in this room, in London, the breath squeezed out of me, sore and gasping, like the fish Adik used to catch, flopping around on the riverbank while they died.

He says he's sorry. He looks at his shoes as he buttons up his jeans and mumbles an apology. At least he wasn't rude or angry, like some of them. At first, I used to get upset. The way they looked at me afterward, and called me names. I thought maybe it was because I wasn't good enough, or sexy enough, or pretty enough, not like the other girls, the older ones from Belarus and Latvia, the blonde ones who could pretend they were Scandinavian. Antonio said he didn't want me in the club, on show to everybody, at least not at first. I learned later it was because he didn't want someone spotting that I was underage.

In my head I am not here, on this dirty mattress in England. In my head I am up above the earth, where the wind howls and the air rushes against my face. Up here I can see the whole of the world turning like a globe: America, Australia, China, India, Africa, Europe, and, all the time, above me, stretching around nearly the whole of the top of the world, Russia. I swoop down low over this country and its dark black forests and blue lakes, its craggy mountains and the endless yellow plains. I fly on and on, farther up into the north, where nobody lives, where there is always frost and snow, to the places where it is so cold you can freeze to death in a second. Where the ice is so white it is blinding. This is where I go in my head while they pay for my body. I figured out in Italy that if I am already frozen inside, no one can ever get in and hurt me.

It's late, the time of night just before it tips over into morning. Three, maybe four o'clock. I feel so tired. I want to sleep, but it's like the Turkish are staying open late just to spite me. I doze on the scruffy sofa in the client lounge, jumping awake every time I hear a door slam. There hasn't been a new client for over half an hour.

The Turkish guys are in the corridor outside, sitting on chairs, smoking. They take turns getting money from the men, and showing them the girls. In fact, they show them photos of us so they can choose who they want. If we're busy they offer them coffee, vodka, and cigarettes while they wait, which all cost extra. Beyond the corridor is another flight of stairs that leads to the door where they come in. I have only seen down from the top of the stairs, when one of the Turkish men took me to the bathroom. At the bottom is a security gate and a heavy blue door with bolts and locks all over it.

I have been thinking about this door. I wonder how long it would take to open it. There are at least two bolts and several locks. And what's on the other side of it? Even in the bedrooms where we take the clients, the windows are boarded over and disguised by heavy velvet curtains so it's not possible to look out. If I stay here I will die, or get sick, or both. This is not like in Italy, where at least if you were hungry Antonio would buy you food. This is not a classy place.

I bury my face in the fabric of the cheap sofa. I feel a weight around my neck like I am being tied to a rock and drowned, pulled deeper and deeper down into the depths where there is no light.

The door below slams with a heavy crash that makes the floor shake. There are voices and footsteps outside. I curl up on the sofa and close my eyes. I hope it's not another client. But then there are raised voices talking in Turkish, one of them sounds excited, like he's trying to explain something to his friends. One of them says the word English and something about a paper. Then suddenly they all laugh and stamp on the

114

floor with their heels and I hear the word for girl and virgin and some whoops and screams. I grit my teeth. I know if it wasn't for me, she wouldn't be here. I hope they will not be hard on her; the first time it always hurts. I remember that. But it's my door that opens and in comes a young, skinny guy. He's got a mop of thick, curly hair that almost looks African and pink, plump lips like a cherub. I haven't seen him before. I watch him through my eyelashes as he walks toward me. He's a lot younger than the others, perhaps somebody's son, somebody's cousin. Maybe sixteen or something, the hairs on his chin haven't even grown in properly.

"Hey." He touches me on the shoulder. "Wake up," he says in English.

I pretend to be really drowsy. "Oh!" I sit up, stretch and yawn, all the time watching him to see how he reacts. He looks bewildered and embarrassed, faintly horrified, and he's staring at the floor. "What's happening?"

He drags his foot across the carpet, his face burning pink. "I —I—Er. Uh-uh . . ." He clears his throat so many times I wonder if there is something wrong with him.

"Did they send you in here?" I whisper.

He nods. I can hear the men outside laughing and whooping. "To be with me?"

He bites his lip and nods again.

"It's okay," I say. "Sit down over here."

He looks up shyly, like he's ashamed. "I don't want to—"

"Me neither."

He sits down cautiously.

"What's your name?"

"Fazil. What's yours?"

"Natasha."

"It—it's my cousin. He works here. You're kind of like

115

my . . . birthday present." He hasn't got a strong Turkish accent, he sounds more English, like Hope.

"Happy birthday, Fazil."

"Thanks." He flicks his hair nervously off his face. "Look, can you like, *pretend* or something? Or tell them I was really good?"

"Okay."

He looks relieved. "Thanks."

I shrug.

"I'm not gay, you know."

"Okay."

"Just in case you thought I was."

"I don't think anything," I say.

"I'm sorry."

"It's okay."

Everybody is sorry. Sorry sorry sorry. Always sorry. Sorry for what? Sorry for spoiling my life? Or sorry they're stupid? Or sorry they can't help wanting sex? There's no point in saying sorry unless you know what for.

"So why are you hanging out with your cousin? If you don't want to be here?" I change the subject.

He shrugs and looks miserable. He tells me that his cousin, Babalan, is part of an important family around here. "He wanted someone to help him out with stuff. So he asked me." He balls his hand into a fist. "My dad makes out like its some great honor, the family sticking together. He doesn't see that he's like a total psycho."

The men outside bang on the door. They want to know if he's finished yet.

"Tell them you're coming," I hiss. "Try to sound out of breath."

"Why?"

"Just do it!"

"I'm coming!" he shouts. When the men outside roar with approval and shout advice and encouragement through the wall he goes bright red, stands up and backs away from me.

He knocks on the door and tells the guys he's finished. Two of them come in, making signs for sex with their arms.

"Good was it?"

"I wouldn't mind a piece of that myself!"

I guess one of them, the fat guy, is Babalan. His friend, the sleazy rat with all his gold jewelry and hip-hop clothes and jeans tucked into heavy Timberland boots, is called Latif.

I smile like I'm enjoying their joke. Like I'm happy and jovial, like the boy is the best lover in the world. The men touch me and grab at me as they're laughing, so I feel like a chicken caught by a fox, trapped and flustered, being played with first, before the fox moves in for the kill.

15

Hope

Oksana. That's what she says her real name is. She says she comes from Russia, but she still won't tell me exactly what's going on. At least she's not still angry with me—just distant and vague again. I know they want us here for sex, but I thought prostitutes *wanted* to do it, and were grown-up and wore loads of makeup and sexy clothes. Thinking about it all makes me feel like I'm falling off the edge of a high cliff.

"It's not so bad for you," I say, turning on my side to look at her back. "At least you are old enough."

"Eh? Old enough?" She turns round.

"I'm only fifteen. It isn't even *legal* for me to have sex." Oksana laughs. "How old do you think I am?"

"I don't know." I look at her for a second. Her face already has hard lines around the eyes. I reckon she's in her late twenties, maybe even thirty. The closer I look at her, the older she seems. "Twenty-three?" I try.

She snorts. "I'm fifteen."

For a moment I don't believe her. It's just another one of her lies, like telling me she was getting married to Zergei. "*Right.*"

"They got me passports that say I am eighteen," she says. "When I left home I was fourteen."

I stare at her. I want to tell her I'm sorry, but it doesn't seem enough. This whole situation is so messed up.

"How—" But before I can finish my question there's a noise

118

outside, the sharp sound of bolts and locks. Fat Burger Man comes in with his friend, a shorter, fitter man with gold rings on his fingers and chains round his neck.

Fat Burger Man throws two T. J. Maxx bags onto Oksana's bed. "You try."

No one moves. Gold Jewelry Man stands by the door and looks at the sleeping Estonians, his nose curling like there's a bad smell.

"*Now*." Fat Burger Man prods Oksana.

She sits up and stares at him, her arms folded. But she is small and puny next to his puffy frame. He picks a bag and shakes it over the floor. Bras, panties, thongs, nightgowns and camisoles slide out in a slippery pile. They look cheap. Bright reds and tacky electric pinks.

"You *try*," he says again, pulling Oksana roughly up by the arm. She shakes him off and bends down to sift through the pile. I don't know what to do, but I don't want him to come near me so I pick up a baby-blue nightgown with fake fluff around the bottom, that's made out of scratchy see-through netting. The kind of thing Mum would say was trashy. I try not to think about her, it only makes my eyes throb with tears. The note I left will have kept her calm initially, but by now I know she will be worried out of her mind and it's my stupid fault. I hope Dad's with her. He can't say that she's making a drama out of a crisis anymore. The police must be looking for me by now. Someone must have seen something, all those nosy women in the store.

The Estonians groan and complain when Fat Burger Man pulls the covers off them.

"You are always sleeping!" he says, except he pronounces it so it sounds like "slipping." He slaps them round their faces, hard.

Lulu gets out of bed. She walks like her legs are soft and her arms flop about at her sides. She looks really stoned. She huffs and mutters something to Ekaterina. They think the underwear is lame too, I can tell.

We all stand there for a moment looking at each other. I wonder what would happen if I said no.

"On! On!" He shoves Oksana in the back.

She grunts and roughly takes off her jacket. "Okay, okay." When she takes off her top I can see her arms and chest are covered with yellowing bruises, her ribs stick out and she's hardly got any boobs at all; suddenly she looks even younger than fifteen. She tosses her hair out of its elastic and tries on one of the pink bras. But it's way too big and the straps keep slipping down. She throws it back on the pile and shouts at him.

"This stuff is no good! Too big!"

He throws the second bag at her.

"ON!"

I step out of my jeans. I wish that I could wash up. I am sticky and dirty. I try to keep my head down, use my arms strategically to hide myself as I pull off my T-shirt. The nightgown is like a huge see-through tent; it comes down below my knees, and the armholes sag over my shoulders. I feel ridiculous.

Fat Burger Man comes over, parts my arms with his hand.

He looks me up and down and nods. Then he puts his hand down my back and yanks off the tag. My skin prickles.

"Nice tits," he says. Inside, I want to die with shame.

Oksana is wearing a bright red all-in-one bodysuit with suspenders that flap around her skinny legs. It fits better than the bra, but it's still too big on her slight frame.

Lulu and Ekaterina are wearing G-strings with black night-gowns over them.

Kaz and Amanda always wear G-strings. They wear them with hiphuggers so the string shows over the top of their jeans.

"Fashionable, isn't it?" Kaz said once, admiring herself in

the mirror, the way the string sat over the hollow at the base of her spine. Thinking about her now, grinning at her own reflection, I feel suddenly ashamed.

"Much big and much cheap," Lulu says, wagging a finger at Fat Burger Man, who shrugs. He grabs her face with his hand, squeezing her chin with his fingers and thumb. He drags her to the mirror and makes her look in it.

"Face!" he says. "Your face!" He grabs a lipstick and puts some on her lips in a shaky line.

Lulu pulls away from him and sneers. But while she fumbles in her bag for her makeup I can see that her hands are trembling.

"Now we go."

"I can't go out like this!" I say, and then hear, the second I've said it, how pointless and prim I sound.

Fat Burger Man talks to his friend. Then they both stare at me and laugh.

"It's okay," Oksana hisses at me. "They don't want you. Not yet anyway."

For a moment I wonder what I've done wrong and the thought that maybe I'm not pretty enough hovers in the corner of my mind. Then I'm scared that I even care.

"Where are they taking you?"

Oksana shrugs. "To work."

Gold Jewelry Man opens the door and ushers them out with extravagant arm gestures.

Fat Burger Man stares at me.

"*Tsok-tsok. Tsok.* Little English chicken," he says, closing the door behind him.

The moment the door is locked I put my clothes on again. My cheeks burn with shame. I know now they only wanted me to get changed so they could look. As I wash my hands in the sink, my skin itches all over. I have to get out of here.

I wonder what time it is. And this thought turns into an obsession. I *have* to know what time it is. I go through all the stuff in the room looking for a clock, a watch.

It's like I can't remember what my life was like before and that makes me feel even more panicky and scared. Suddenly, all there is in the world is this room, this life, and everything that has gone on before it is just a blurry dream.

Eventually, I find the cracked face of a digital watch by Lulu's bed: 1:21. Lunchtime. Lunchtime . . . Wednesday, no it must be *Thursday*. I'm sure I've been gone for at least two whole days. I find a scrap of newspaper and write it down. School starts back next week. I wonder what Kaz and Amanda are doing. If they know I'm missing yet. I lie back on the bed, clutching the watch, and sleep fitfully all afternoon.

I'm groggy and sleepy. It's 3:56 according to the cheap screen on Lulu's watch. I wonder where Oksana has been all this time. I don't know how much longer I can cope, being in this room on my own. But then the stairs creak and there is the sound of voices outside.

Fat Burger Man comes in first carrying a huge TV; behind him, Oksana and Lulu and Gold Jewelry Man and someone I haven't seen before: a boy with a thin fuzz of hair on his lip. He slouches against the wall with his hands in his pockets staring at me.

Oksana looks pale and exhausted. She flops on the bed next to me and closes her eyes.

"What happened?"

"Ngh." She waves a hand at me. "Talking later."

Lulu is bitching at Fat Burger Man, in Turkish I think. He shouts back at her and puts the TV on a bedside cabinet.

"Where did they take you?"

"Downstairs," Oksana mumbles into the bed.

Gold Jewelry Man has got a DVD player and there's a lot of frowning and quick talking as he tries to figure out with Fat Burger Man how they're going to plug it in.

"What's going on?"

Oksana sits up and stares at me. "I don't know!" she shouts. "Stop talking to me!"

"I'm sorry, I was only—"

"*You* are sorry!" She's getting a bit hysterical now. "We are *all* sorry! Everybody is sorry!" She points around the room.

"I'm sor—it's okay." I don't want her to get upset, not right now, not while *they're* here. "*Shhhh.*"

But she doesn't shut up. She keeps screaming, "I'm sorry! I'm sorry!" Her voice is hoarse and dry and she screams and screams until Gold Jewelry Man stops what he's doing and slaps her. He twists her arm behind her back until she shouts and he pushes her headfirst onto the bed. Then he stops and goes back to what he was doing, just like nothing happened. Oksana lies still, her face buried in the pillow, and for a moment I worry that he might have killed her, but then I can see her back moving gently up and down.

I get that sickly feeling again like I got in the car. Like I've gone down in an elevator too quickly, like the world around me is made of water, like I'm trapped inside a bad dream. I sit on the bed and chew my fingernails and wish the boy in the corner would stop staring at us like we're animals in the zoo.

Finally they get a picture on the screen. Fat Burger Man turns the TV around so we can all see it. He pulls Oksana's hair to make her sit up.

"Now you watch." He points with a flourish to the screen. The menu for *Showgirls* comes up. At first I think it must be

123

porn, but when the credits roll I can see it's a proper movie with Gina Gershon in it.

"Come on, baby." He sits heavily on the bed and puts his arm round Oksana. "I look after you." She tenses, but she doesn't say anything.

He fast forwards the film so I don't really get a sense of the story, except that it's about Las Vegas strippers and topless dancers.

Then he pauses on a scene of women dancing on a huge glittering stage with explosions and fake volcanoes and loud music.

"See?" he says, pointing as the women go through a really hyper and athletic topless dance routine. "Like that! *That* is how you dance!"

He rewinds to the start of the scene, making the women dance backward, so Gina Gershon's character goes back inside her volcano instead of coming out of it. I wonder how she doesn't get burned with all the fireworks going on around her.

"You do it!" Fat Burger Man points at Lulu. "You copy."

She curls her lip and gives him a disbelieving glare.

He stands up and plays the scene again. He claps his hands. "Come on!"

Oksana stands up, slowly, like an old lady with stiff joints. She winces as she moves her hips. I stand next to her and stretch my arms. I feel like I'm trying to copy one of Mum's exercise DVDs.

Lulu whimpers when he comes near her, but he grabs her by the neck of her T-shirt and pulls her in front of the TV screen. "Dance!"

"Have they got a club or something?"

"No." Oksana furrows her brow in concentration. "Private dancing."

Private dancing. I can't do that. Not like on the video

anyway. Besides, I don't want to learn how to walk like a crab and thrust my crotch at a man, especially not in front of Fat Burger Man and Mad Staring Boy.

Lulu sways around making vague gestures at the screen. The routine is finished by the time she gets even one move right. He rewinds the scene.

"Again." He claps his hands. This time she manages a few arm movements.

"In the morning you will show me." He pats Lulu on the butt. "Too fat," he says as he walks past, even though I can see that this is not true.

As they leave the room, Mad Staring Boy says something to Fat Burger Man, which makes him laugh. He claps the boy hard on the back, making him stumble and hang his head.

After they've gone we watch the film. It's not very good, and the bright sparkly settings and clean peachy skin of the characters make our room seem even more disgusting.

Oksana stares at the screen without moving. I don't even think she's really watching it. Lulu lights a cigarette and curls her knees up to her chest.

"You're not fat," I say.

She looks at me and smiles and her face softens—she doesn't look so scary and hard.

I say thank you, but I don't know why.

She waves me away with her hand. "Don't be thank you. You don't know. I am bad persons." She gets up and goes over to her bed.

Oksana snorts. "You are stupid," she says, "but not bad. It's *them* who is bad." She jabs a finger at the door. "We are just carrying the badness for them, like a heavy load."

16

Oksana

"He's not coming back," I said to Adik one day. He was throwing stones at an empty can, trying to get it to roll down the street.

Adik scrunched his face up. "Yes he *is*."

"How do you know? Dimitri and Kolya don't think he's coming back."

"Because he said so."

"And you believe what he says?"

"Yes!" He hit the can, sending it skittering across the street. "He said he wanted to do business here."

"Business? What business is there here? No one has any money."

Adik shrugged. "He said there is always money, you just have to know where to look for it."

"Where is there always money? Under the rocks and stones? Like treasure?"

"I don't know!" Adik sounded irritated.

Since Tommy and the fight, we hadn't really been getting along very well. Just because we kissed once, he was always bragging about it, like now I was his girlfriend or something. Plus he'd become like an irritating fly, always buzzing about himself. As if he was special just because Tommy gave *him* a stupid dollar. Like it was a sign from heaven that he was going to get out of here. Every time he talked about it my heart was heavy. It wasn't *fair*.

*

It was a gray, boring kind of day when the noise of an engine buzzed in the distance. Adik pricked up his ears like a guard dog, and even Viktor stopped whining as the sound got closer. I could tell it was a new car; the way the engine purred instead of chugging and backfiring.

"He's back!"

Adik ran in the direction of the sound, waving his arms. "Over here!"

It was a BMW this time, with tinted windows and chrome trim.

"Hey," Tommy said, lowering the window and leaning out. His hair was different, brushed flat and cut neatly behind his ears, and he was wearing a suit and tie. There was someone in the passenger seat. A bald man who was also wearing a suit. He stared at us without saying anything.

"Which way to the concrete factory?"

Adik pointed the way. "They thought you weren't coming back," he said, "but I told them you were." He stuck his chest out proudly.

Tommy laughed and nodded. "*Spasibo*. You are a good boy." He held out a note with his fingers. Another dollar bill.

When he was gone Adik held it up to me triumphantly. "See?" he said.

The next day I couldn't find Adik anywhere. I waited outside the store nearly all day, my head full of questions. It was getting dark when I gave up on him and started to trudge home with Viktor pulling on my arm and whining about being hungry.

"Surprise!"

I nearly jumped out of my skin. Adik's pale face glowed in the dusk. He was giggling and grinning.

127

"What's wrong with you?" I hit him upside the head. "I waited for you all day."

He ducked away from me. "I was busy," he said, puffing out his chest and putting his shoulders back. Even though he was skinny, he was nearly taller than me now. "I was *working*." He giggled again and staggered slightly into the wall.

"Are you drunk?"

"Maybe a little."

I grabbed Viktor's hand. "Then I'm going *home*."

But he stood in front of me. "Don't go," he said. "I've got presents." He pulled a red packet out of his bag. I took it and tried to spell out the writing. Maltesers, European candy.

"Where did you get this?"

"Tommy got it at the airport in Berlin. He said he's going to get me a job. He says he knows a man in Germany looking for boys like me."

"To do what?"

Adik shrugged. "Work."

"What kind of work?" I wondered if it was the kind of work I could do too. "Do they need anyone else?"

"Ask Tommy." He opened the packet of candy and gave a handful to Viktor. Viktor shoved them in his mouth all at once, smearing chocolate round his lips.

"Eat!" Adik said, trying to give me some too.

"Get off." I pushed his hand impatiently, spilling candies all over the ground. Viktor pulled away from me and picked them up, even the ones that had fallen in the puddles and in the gutter.

He said he'd been with Tommy all day, helping him to "take care of business."

"What kind of business? Business where you get drunk?"

But he just shrugged and told me that girls didn't understand men's business and, anyway, he was fed up with me asking so many questions.

"Well I'm fed up with you!" I said. "And all your bullshit about Tommy."

I didn't want to hear any more. I yanked Viktor by the arm and walked away from him.

"Oksana!" He ran after me. "Don't be mad at me."

I continued to walk. "Why not? You're very annoying."

I didn't look back. I stomped home faster and faster, dragging Viktor by the arm behind me. He started crying, so I had to stop and carry him. When I turned around to pick him up I couldn't see Adik anywhere and I was disappointed. I really wanted him to follow me. To tell me it would be okay, that he'd fix it so I could go away with him too. That I could leave Father and Viktor and my miserable life and start somewhere new. After all, if it could happen to him, why not to me?

I promised myself then that I was going to get away. Whatever it took. I wasn't going to be left behind to shrivel up into a bag lady; all the years of struggle to stay alive leathering my skin, shrinking my bones, turning my eyes into raisins. I wasn't going to be like Baba Droski or Mrs. Borodovna, or even become a furred-up snob like Tetya Svetlana. I wanted a different kind of life. I wanted not to worry every day about whether there was food, not to have Viktor to take care of, not to wake up in the morning and feel huge pressure on my head because my mother was dead and now there was no one else to keep our family together.

"Hey!"

I was so lost in my own thoughts I didn't even hear the car approaching.

"You not talking to me?" Tommy smiled so I could see his white teeth. "Want a ride?" He opened the door, patted the passenger seat with his hand.

For a second I hesitated. Thought that maybe I should just

go home, try to find something to cook for Father and Viktor. But then I got in.

"What are you doing here?" I asked, putting Viktor on my lap, trying to keep his dirty hands off the shiny dashboard. Tommy didn't seem to notice. When he smiled his eyes crinkled around the edges. I could see the rough stubble on his chin; he looked like a real man.

"Investing," he said, concentrating on the road.

"In the factory?"

"Maybe."

I told him to turn down the road toward the apartments. He had to steer hard to avoid the potholes and the puddles. "You live around here?"

He slowed the car and looked up through the windshield at the apartments, the tall square blocks of windows and crumbling balconies.

A skinny cat darted through the garbage. No one ever came to take the garbage away. Mostly it sat at the bottom of the block rotting, or it got scavenged and reused, or burned up in fires.

People were watching, I could tell; curtains twitched, a few people stared at us over their balconies. Not many people had cars, let alone ones that worked. There were only a few empty shells that had been abandoned when they broke down, old cars that only worked if you pushed them.

I felt ashamed, bringing him here.

"They should blow them up," he said, looking at me. "This is no place for anyone to live."

A part of me wanted to shout at him to go away because I thought I should defend our apartment, where our mother used to live. We were a proud family, we didn't like to have people look down their noses at us. But another side of me was relieved.

"I know," I said. "I hate my life."

He looked sad then, and brushed a strand of hair from my forehead. "You are too young to hate your life."

"Adik says you're getting him a job," I started. "Can you get me a job too? Please?"

"How old are you? Really?"

"Fourteen soon."

He shook his head. "You're too young. I can't . . ." He stopped and bit his lip. "Maybe in a while, but we need papers and that kind of thing. You wait until I come back. Maybe I will build a supermarket here; I make jobs, I make money. Maybe you can have a job then."

"But Adik—"

"He is a boy. It is different for boys."

"How is it different?" The comment annoyed me. It seemed like it was always different for boys. If they could go anywhere, do anything, how come I couldn't?

"You'll find out when you're older," he said, leaning across me to open the car door. "See you later, little chicken."

I ran inside with Viktor, jumping over the puddles as quick as I could, my face shadowed like a sunset. I couldn't believe it, he thought I was too young.

Inside, I looked at my face in the mirror in the bathroom, my blunt hair that I cut myself with the kitchen scissors, my dirty, scrubby cheeks. In the mirror I didn't look young, I looked like a shadowy picture of my mother and Baba Droski, with Dad's thick eyebrows. I looked wrong, I knew I did. I needed grooming, I needed makeup, clothes, perfume, shoes. I needed to look my age.

In the corner of Mother and Father's bedroom was a painted wooden box. Now chipped and faded gray, it was once black and covered with posies of bright pink and red flowers with green leaves. Mother said it belonged to my great-grandfather,

Papa Yudaev. It was Mother's wedding box. In it she kept her wedding shawl and pressed flowers from her corsage and all her jewelry and makeup. She said that one day, when I got married, the box would be mine. She said it had been in the family so long that Papa Yudaev had carried it when he was running from the Germans. "See that chip on the side? That's from a German bullet."

Father laughed at her when she told me that story. He said it was far more likely that Papa Yudaev dropped it when he was drunk. She didn't speak to him for nearly a week after he said that. She said she didn't mind him disrespecting her, but she did mind him disrespecting her family and all that they had lived through. He said he was only joking but she sulked anyway, until a few days later he came back from work with a bunch of fresh sunflowers and cornflowers that he'd picked himself from the fields and said he was sorry for being a jerk. Mother's face softened then and she let him grab her around the waist and kiss her, and I ran out of the room making faces because I was only seven years old and didn't understand anything about the world.

These memories surprised me as I ran my hands across the flaking varnish. After she died, Father threw out all her clothes, even though I told him we could use them. He said he didn't want them hanging in the closet reminding him of what he had lost. But he didn't throw away her box. I told myself it was because he was saving it for me. That he'd remembered that Mom meant to keep it for my wedding day. So he wouldn't mind if I borrowed some of her makeup before I got married, especially if I told him about Adik and Tommy and the work in Germany.

Inside the box was a tattered satin clutch bag, the green material frayed and worn from years of her fingers opening and closing the clasp. It still smelled of her, which suddenly brought her back, warm and close, so I could see the imprerfections in the fabric of her homemade sweater and the way she stretched her lips when she was putting on lipstick. The purse still contained one bright red lipstick, a compact with a small smear of face powder, an eye pencil, some bright pink blush and several eye shadows in different shades of blue.

"Look at you!" His mouth was crunched, angry. "What do you think you look like?"

I thought I looked good. I had spent hours in front of the mirror, applying and then reapplying the makeup. I had drawn straight lines under my eyes, put a stripe of blue on my eyelids and under my eyebrows and used the lipstick really carefully to fill in my lips without spilling any over the edge.

"Wipe it off!" He tore a corner off a newspaper and threw it at me.

"NO!"

I folded my arms and stared at him. What did he know about being stuck with Viktor all day? About being the only one who ever seemed to worry about where the next meal was coming from?

"Your mother would be ashamed of you."

That accusation hurt, but I wasn't going to give in. "I don't care!" I shouted back. "She's dead!"

It was like a storm had blown up in my head, angry black clouds of frustration and resentment.

"I'm going out!"

"Where?"

"Out."

"No you're not, you're staying here!"

But I was on the right side of the kitchen, nearest the door. I turned around and made a run for it, down the steps, with him on the landing bellowing and calling my name and telling me how I was a no-good daughter and why didn't I dress nicely like other girls? Which I thought was really mean, especially as we never had enough money to buy new clothes. I tried not to listen. I could hear Viktor crying from the kitchen. He hated it when people shouted. Father hadn't even given me a chance to explain, to tell him about Adik and Tommy and the job in Germany, or remind him that soon I would be fourteen.

Adik found me in the alleyway next to the garbage bins for the store. Because I'd been crying, the eye pencil had leaked down my face in black streaks.

"You look like a bear," he said. He was wearing a new pair of pants: clean, dark blue jeans, sneakers that were as white as fresh snow and a navy sport jacket made out of this new material that was soft and still a hundred percent waterproof. He said it was the kind of coat football managers wore on the sidelines.

"Where did you get those?"

"Tommy bought them for me."

"Bought them for you? Why did he do that?" I wiped my eyes with my sweater, and smeared a streak of eyeshadow all over my sleeve.

He frowned like he wasn't sure how to answer this question. "Look!" He pulled something out of his pocket, a little purple book, and he flipped it open.

GUNTHER HAAS, it said next to a photo of him and it gave his age as eighteen.

"That's not your name."

"*Duh*. Tommy knows this guy who's got a computer. He made it for me."

He put it in one of the pockets in his trousers. "I'm leaving tomorrow."

"*Tomorrow?!*" That was too soon. I got the same feeling

I had when Father told me that Mother had died, like the ground underneath me had shifted and turned to water and that nothing would ever be safe anymore.

Adik shrugged. "He wants me to start right away. The sooner I make money, the sooner I come back."

He puffed himself up, trying to make himself big, like he was really eighteen. But to me he still looked like Adik, the skinny rat who had lousy hair and worn-out shoes and dirty hands. He told me that Tommy was coming to get him to drive him to the border.

"Cool," I managed. I could feel my lip starting to wobble, my face getting tight and hot, all the words that I wanted to say to him caught in my throat. But I didn't want him to pity me like I was just some little kid. "Take care."

"Hey! Don't be sad. It's not like I'm dead. I'm coming back."

"I'm not sad!" I stood up and blinked away the tears. A familiar knot of resentment tightened in my belly. "I'm *glad* you're going! Now I don't have to listen to your bullshit anymore!"

"*Oksana!*"

But I turned away from him and shrugged like I didn't care.

"Don't you want to say good-bye?" he called after me.

"No!" I shouted back. I kept on walking down the road, one foot after the other. I don't know why, but I felt like I was in some crazy fight with him in my head, that at all costs I didn't want him to win.

Mikki and Kolya watched him go, running up the road after the car. They said Tommy let Adik drive, at least until they reached the edge of town, where the tin road signs told you how many hundreds of miles it was to get to Moscow, and there was the sign to the factory that Adik and Kolya had put on backward

135

so that anyone who tried to find it would drive for ages in the wrong direction.

"Man he was so slow!"

Kolya giggled. "I mean he drove like he was on a donkey!"

"I could have walked faster!"

"Maybe he didn't want to crash it," I said, imagining him sitting up in the driving seat as tall as he could, arms locked in front of him, inching the car carefully forward.

Mikki and Kolya scoffed at this idea. They said that any fool could drive and what was the point of a performance engine if you didn't go fast? "Are you stupid or what?" Kolya said, turning up his nose and sneering at me. He and Dimitri had recently gotten into sniffing glue and they had turned nasty and spotty, their eyes dead and glassy. I didn't trust them anymore. I huddled into my jacket and ignored them. I knew then for sure that as soon as Viktor was at school, I was out of here. Even if it meant I had to walk all the way.

17

Hope

In the morning they bring us breakfast. Bacon rolls and lukewarm cups of tea in cheap foam cups. I've hardly eaten anything since they brought me here. I've been so scared and confused it's like my stomach has got stuck together and even though I know I should be really hungry, I can only take two bites out of the stale, crumbly roll and greasy bacon. I give it to Oksana who takes it straightaway and eats it in nearly two bites, her cheeks puffing out like a hamster.

Mad Staring Boy is lurking in the corridor with his hands in his pockets while Fat Burger Man and his gold jewelry mate bring in our breakfast, all smiles like we should be happy to see them, like they're being good guys, looking after us.

"What time is it?" I ask.

Gold Jewelry Man glares at me, but doesn't say anything, even though he has a big gold watch on his wrist.

I know it must be daytime, because thin slivers of light shine round the edges of the drywall.

"Time for work!" Fat Burger Man laughs, clapping his hands together.

Oksana groans and flops back on her bed. Fat Burger Man stares at her but she ignores him, gets back under the covers and closes her eyes.

"Get up!" He lumbers over to her bed and yanks her by the ankle. "I say GET UP!"

He pulls her onto the floor and kicks her in the stomach so she yells and curls up like a worm. A few seconds later she coughs and throws up her breakfast onto the carpet.

This seems to make him even more angry. "Clean up!" he says. He bends down and grabs her hair, pulling her upright. "Clean up, pig!"

Lulu and Ekaterina get changed into their nightgowns. I don't know what to do. Mad Staring Boy has come closer, watching from the doorway and frowning. He catches my eye and puts a finger to his lips and shakes his head. I don't know what he means, but I quickly look down at the bed and pick at a thread that's escaping from the mattress.

Oksana's crying now. Even though she's not making a sound. Her cheeks are wet as she bends over to clean the carpet with a cheap scrap of pink toilet paper. My whole body fizzes with nervous energy. I wish I could just bounce about the room like in a computer game, knocking the men out with power punches so Oksana and I can escape. But Fat Burger Man seems to grow bigger every time I look at him.

I can't believe the police haven't found me yet. But if I think about it too much it just makes me depressed. We were in the trunk of the car so no one would have seen us, and now we're in this place that feels like it's on the other side of the world. I wish I'd left some clues: footprints, a trail of breadcrumbs. Even if they figure out that it was Zergei who took us, he's dead now, and I can't imagine what they did to his body. And if they do find him, how are they going to work out where I am from that anyway? I try not to think about this because it makes me feel dizzy and ill, like I'm looking over the edge of a long dark drop.

The boy comes closer, grabs Fat Burger Man by the elbow and asks him something, his eyebrows knitted together. Fat

138

Burger Man laughs at him and grabs at his crotch and shakes his head. The boy looks embarrassed and shrugs his shoulders.

"Come on! Come on, people!" Fat Burger Man says thickly, turning round and clapping his hands together like he learned his English from a dance-mix CD.

I don't know what to do. I don't know if he means me too, and I'm not getting changed again just so they can watch me. He comes over to me like he's read my thoughts, his smile showing yellow, uneven teeth.

"You are making us much trouble," he says, grabbing my chin between his finger and thumb. "I deal with you later."

I glance at Oksana. She's putting on makeup, halfheartedly rubbing foundation on her cheeks, all the time watching us out of the corner of her eye.

"Okay," I say, my heart thumping so fast I think I might faint. Then they all traipse out, Fat Burger Man closing and locking the door behind him. I want to tell them all to get lost, but I don't dare. I'm such a stupid coward. I should have jumped off that roof when I had the chance. Mum was right. I am hopeless. If I was clever and brave I wouldn't be here at all.

That thought makes me cry all over again, wet little sobs that make me feel even more small and stupid and like I can never sort anything on my own. I lie back on the bed and stare at where the window should be. I can still feel the bruises on my wrists from where Oksana pulled me up off the roof. I know I would have fallen if she hadn't grabbed me.

As I think this, the sun must have come out, as wide, bright shafts of sunlight escape round the edges of the drywall on to the floor, showing the dirt and dust in forensic detail. They can't keep it out, I think. And for some reason I find that thought comforting: that even in the dark places, where they try to shut it out, light still shines between the cracks.

139

There has to be another way out of here. I lie back on the bed and try to think straight. I need a plan for both of us.

The tapping is timid, but it still makes me sit up, clutching the thin blanket round my neck. The light has faded to a dull gray and there is the patter of heavy rain on the window outside. Then there's another tap, louder this time.

I can't think who's bothering to knock. Most of the time they just fling open the door.

"Hello?"

The door opens and Mad Staring Boy peeps his head through the gap.

I pull the blanket closer round my neck. I wonder what he wants with me. I push myself away from him, into the wall, knees up to my chest. If he tries to touch me, I'll kick him.

He shuts the door and creeps toward me, pressing a finger to his lips. "*Shhhh*. They're downstairs." His accent is English, which is unexpected, and suddenly comforting. "You're Hope, right?"

"Ye-*es*. Who are you?"

"Babalan and Latif, those men downstairs, they're my cousins." He stands at the end of the bed, fiddling with the zipper on his jacket.

"And?"

"My name is Fazil." He sticks out his hand awkwardly, like he wants me to shake it. I ignore him so instead he pulls a scrap of newspaper out of his pocket. "Is this you?"

I look at it, my heart sinking. It's a picture of me from when I was like thirteen, by the pool, smiling and waving at the camera, my hair blowing in strands behind me in the breeze.

"Why did Mum choose that photo?!" I say out loud, outraged; all that skin showing makes me cringe:

Concerns Mount for Wealthy Businessman's Missing Daughter

Police are increasingly concerned about the whereabouts of Hope Tasker, daughter of former New Businessman of the Year Mr. Derek Tasker (54). Hope (14) left a note for her parents to say she was heading to London for the day but never returned. Her parents say this behavior is out of character for the normally "quiet and lovely" girl, who was supposed to be starting school again at the exclusive Norwich High School for Girls next week.

Police are keen to talk to anyone who might have encountered Hope on their journey to London on Tuesday, and are concentrating their inquiries on the Norwich-to-London train service, on which they believe Miss Tasker may have been a passenger.

"We are currently reviewing the CCTV footage from the station," PC Keith Evans, spokesperson for the Norfolk Constabulary, said in a press conference this morning. "But at this stage we are keeping a very open mind and are keen to speak to anyone who might have seen her. We are appealing to members of the public across the country, but especially in Norfolk and London, who might have seen something suspicious, or someone they know acting suspiciously, to get in touch as a matter of urgency."

"Yes, it's me." I swallow the lump in my throat and hand the paper back to him. I feel relieved and then scared and then weirdly guilty for causing such a fuss. "But that picture doesn't even look like me anymore."

He shakes his head. "My cousin . . . he's into all sorts of shit but I never thought . . ." He looks scared. "They bought you by mistake. They got conned into thinking you were one of *them*." He nods at the empty beds. "They've been trying to figure out what to do with you. And now this story is in the papers . . . They've got guns, you know. And like these big samurai swords and stuff. They're crazy."

I get out of bed and stand up. I'm the same height as him. I reckon I could push him over if I had to. Blood thumps through my veins.

"Then let me go."

There's a noise downstairs, someone shouting. He jumps like he's been burned.

"I've got to go," he says.

But this could be my chance, I realize.

"Call the police!"

"No!"

"You don't have to say who you are!" I follow him as he backs away toward the door.

"I—I *can't*. I mean, he might be insane, but he's *family*. And what if—"

I touch him on the shoulder. "*Please.*"

"Leave me alone!" he growls suddenly, brushing me off. "Go away!" And he slams the door.

I get really scared again after he's gone and start to hyperventilate till I think I might pass out. My body won't stop trembling so I hold my breath and try to count to five before I let it out again. Why did he tell me all that stuff if he didn't want to help me? Now all I can think is that I'm going to get my head cut off with a big samurai sword, or be slashed to pieces like in a horror movie.

I lose track of time a bit after that, and the next thing I know Fat Burger Man is standing in the doorway, taking up space and grumbling to someone standing behind him.

"You," he says, waving at me, "come with me. *Now.*"

I don't move a muscle.

"Come now." He walks closer to the bed, grabs my arm above the elbow and pulls me up.

Fazil is in the corridor. He looks away as I let myself be pulled up.

"Where are you taking me?" I try to level the panic that rises in my voice.

"Not far, not far," Fat Burger Man says. Fazil said he was called Babalan or something, but I don't care what his name is. He still looks like a fat burger in his tan leather jacket and greasy white T-shirt.

He pushes me through the corridor and down the flight of stairs to the next floor. Here the light is much brighter, the carpets a thick sea of pink and the walls a badly painted yellowish color. From the landing, I can see down another narrow flight of steps to another door: a blue metal door with lots of locks on it, and in front of that an iron gate that looks as if it's locked shut with a padlock. Like a prison entrance or something.

"Quick, quick." Fat Burger Man prods me in the back. I don't want to think about what they're going to do to me now.

There are pictures in cheap clip frames, cheesy shots of Jenna Jameson and Pamela Anderson in underwear or swimsuits. Fat Burger Man nearly knocks them off the walls, he is so wide.

"In here." He shoves me into the door and squashes against me as he leans over to turn the handle.

Inside is Gold Jewelry Man—Latif—and a video camera. He's pinned a white sheet to the wall and put a chair in front of it.

"Sit down," he says.

In the lens of the camera I can see my reflection, magnified, turned upside down. Instinctively, I fold my arms across my body. I hope they don't want me to do any sexy dancing.

Fat Burger Man mumbles something in Turkish and leaves

the room, slamming the door behind him. Fazil leans against it, his hands behind his back.

"Okay, smile!"

I grimace.

"No," Latif says, "like you are happy."

"I would be happy if you let me go home," I say.

He waves his hands at me like I'm stupid. "Soon, soon." He presses a button on the top of the camera. "Now I want you to tell me that you are okay and have food and sleep."

"What?"

"You must talk to your parents." He points at the camera. "They will give us some money for taking care of you and then you go home. Simple."

"You're asking my mum and dad for money?"

He nods. "Of course. We have to pay for you, English girl, so how else are we getting our money back? They pay, you go home. Simple."

A small flutter of relief and hope dances around in my chest. Mum and Dad can afford to pay to get me back. "How much?"

"Two million pounds."

"But they don't have that much!"

Two million? I know Dad has made a lot of money recently, but it's not *that* much.

He shrugs. "Your father is a businessman. Businessmen can always get money. Businessmen make best customers."

It takes a moment for the insinuation to sink in. "My father would never come somewhere—somewhere like here!"

Latif laughs. "How do you know? Now, you smile and talk to the camera."

The way that he laughs like he's aware of everything in the world makes me really angry. My eyes itch and my bottom lip wobbles.

"If you want me not to kill you, you will not cry!" He stares at me. "I am not joking."

Fazil says something then, fast and urgent, and Latif pauses, then grunts. "I am going to get breakfast and when I come back you will be smiling."

The minute he leaves the room I start to cry, properly now. I just want to be *home*.

Fazil puts his hand on my shoulder. "It's okay," he says.

I shrug him off. But he grabs my hand, presses something into my palm.

"No. No. *Look*."

Two bronze keys. One for our room and one for the gate, he says. He took them from the office downstairs. "Do it later tonight when they're finished. Babalan and Latif are going out so they'll probably close up early. Someone will be watching down here and there's a CCTV camera outside the front door so make sure you sneak away when no one is looking at it. Wait until they go to sleep around five in the morning. Be quick, and don't get caught." He folds my fingers round the key. "I'm sorry," he says. "That's all I can do."

"Okay, thank you," I snuffle.

"And stop crying. Just do what he tells you. Don't make it *worse*."

"What about the others?"

"What others?"

"Natasha; the other girls."

He looks at his shoes. "You're different from them," he says. "But if you want to tell them that's your business."

"Don't you care?! It's not like they want to be here either!"

He looks uncomfortable and lights a cigarette and starts whining about how things aren't working out for him the way he wanted. His father took him out of school before he could take his qualifying exams, to make him work for Babalan. "I just want to go to college and learn about computers."

Paranoid, he checks the camera to make sure it isn't recording. "Babalan knows I'm not really up for all this. He's like watching me the whole time. One day soon, he's going to expect me to beat someone up and I won't be able to do it. Then he'll say all this stuff about me, come after me and my family too. He did that to my other cousin. He started a whole feud for no reason except that he felt like it. My uncle is in Turkey hiding now because he is so afraid of him."

Then the sound of a door slamming downstairs startles him and he goes back to the door and stands at attention.

"If you get caught, don't tell them it was me that helped you. *Please*," he hisses just before Latif comes back in eating a kebab out of a wrap of white paper. He's got grease all round his lips as he squints into the camera to get the shot right. The keys burn in my pocket. Tonight we will get out of here. The thought is like taking lungfuls of fresh air.

"Come on now," Latif says. "Smile for Daddy."

18

Oksana

I wonder now why we never asked what it was the man in Germany wanted Adik to do for him. It was like all the *stuff*—the car, the clothes, the money—dazzled us like the bright sun. Now that I know what it is that happens, how scared and mean and cold and hungry the whole world is, I am frightened for him. But when I first got that postcard, tattered and worn by the long journey through the mail, I threw it under the bed.

We rarely got any mail, unless it was bills or the occasional letter from Tetya Svetlana in which she told us how good life was in Moscow and how Yaris had just been promoted and how I should keep studying hard at my English so I could marry well and be like her—escape the dreary countryside and get a good job, husband, and a nice apartment with working heat and a microwave. Sometimes she slipped a few roubles in between the thin sheets of writing paper, which meant that I checked for the mail every day, even though most of the time there was nothing.

When I opened the battered green mailbox at the bottom of our apartment the day Adik's postcard came, at first I thought maybe it was a joke. The pictures of the men in red coats with tall furry hats, and important-looking buildings and statues, seemed strange and out of place in our heap-of-shit block. England? I thought he was going to Germany. His handwriting was

147

big and scrawly, like he was trying hard to hold the pen steady. And no explanation, just the words *Write me* and two kisses.

Write him? I didn't know where to start. I could have written him a whole book about how much I wanted to leave too, and how unfair it was that he went first, and how annoyed I was he didn't even send any money, not one rouble. If he wanted me to write to him, he should have sent me the money for a stamp.

So the postcard stayed under the bed with the dust and the mice, and life went on like normal all through the winter, with me and Viktor stuck in the apartment most of the time because it was too cold to go outside—the ground was thick with snow and ice and we didn't have enough warm clothes.

Our apartment was falling apart around us. A big crack had appeared on the wall of the kitchen and the roof had started leaking, a brown seeping in the corner, which made the paper fall off the walls, showing the moldy concrete underneath.

Mother would have made a fuss about that, got Father to bring back some concrete from work so we could fix it, or she would have found some scraps of material to hide it, maybe a woolen rug or a sheet.

Every day was the same: get up at five with Father, feed Viktor, go back to sleep, wake up again freezing cold because the radiators didn't work right, amuse Viktor, stare out of the filthy windows at the suffocating snow and wonder whether Father would have to sleep at the factory again; then, later, when Viktor has whined that he wants to go outside, and scribbled on the wall with my eye pencil, try to make supper out of one moldy carrot and a potato. Go to sleep again, hungry and cold and not tired. Lie in the dark listening to Viktor breathing, to the distant sounds of shouting and banging and *popsa* on a tiny radio, and wonder for how long my life would be like this.

Tommy came back in the spring. When the snow had melted and the frozen ground had turned into puddles of mud and slippery grass, and I had rescued Adik's postcard from under the bed and started writing letters to him in my head. This time he had a 4x4. A silver Land Rover, brand new, although it was already covered with dirt from the road.

I had taken Viktor out for some fresh air and we were standing around on the concrete underneath the awning of the store when he swept in. The car slid to a slick stop, spraying the sidewalk and Viktor and me with muddy water.

"Sorry!" He jumped out, all smiles, with a handful of napkins.

"It's okay," I said, snatching the napkins from him. I didn't want him to look at my legs, the purple tights I was wearing, a Christmas present from Tetya Svetlana that were already going saggy at the knees. I wiped some mud off Viktor's face and tried to clean my boots, but they were already so filthy there didn't seem to be any point.

Almost immediately, Mikki and Kolya came running up the street, pawing the car, crowding around Tommy like he was Santa Claus who had come with sacks of Christmas presents. I tried to fade into the background, meaning to sneak off around the corner and go home.

"Oksana!" Tommy came over and grabbed me by the wrist. "Don't you want to go shopping?"

"Shopping?"

"Yeah." He shrugged. "I'm driving into town. I thought you might like a ride."

"But—" I pointed at Viktor. "And I don't have any money."

"No worries." He reached into his pocket and pulled out a

149

shiny leather wallet. He unfolded a thick wedge of notes and counted out over a hundred roubles.

"Hey, boys, you'll look after Viktor this afternoon? What do you say? Fifty now and fifty when I get back, and you make sure nothing happens to him and I'll give you some extra?"

Kolya snatched Viktor's hand. "Like my brother!" he said.

For a second I thought about saying no. I knew Kolya couldn't be trusted; he would probably spend all the money on glue and then leave Viktor somewhere out in the cold, or worse, lock him in a shed until I came back. But the fact that Tommy had asked me, and not one of the boys, made me feel wanted, special.

Viktor grumbled and pulled away from Kolya, looking up at me with his soft, childish eyes.

"I'm sorry," I said to him. "I have to go somewhere right now. Kolya and Mikki will look after you."

He shook his head and crunched his face like he was going to start crying, but I turned away from him.

"It's okay," I said, walking toward the 4x4. At the time I didn't understand why my feet felt so heavy, why every step I took toward Tommy felt like I was walking through glue. Now I think it must have been my mother, trying to stop me, clinging onto my legs with ghostly arms.

The Land Rover was so high off the ground it was like being a queen. The road seemed small and the horizon huge as we bumped our way toward town. Tommy chain-smoked Marlboro Reds and put a Sting compilation on the CD player.

"Cool, huh?" he said, watching me touch the thick moulded plastic and shiny fittings.

"Yeah." I'd never been in anything like it before. I imagined it was the kind of luxury only presidents and Americans could have.

"So, where d'you want to work?"

Work? My heart leaped. "I thought we were going shopping?"

"Well, after that."

I thought for a minute, a collage of all the countries I had ever heard about swimming in front of me. Germany, Holland, England, Italy, America . . .

"London," I said finally.

He laughed. "Everyone wants to work in London now."

"Adik went to London," I said.

"Adik?" He furrowed his brow like he was trying to remember something.

"Yeah. He said you were taking him to Berlin. Now he's in London."

"Is he?" He turned a corner.

"He sent me a postcard." I pulled the card out of my pocket, unfolded it and held it up so he could see.

"Oh." For a moment he looked almost . . . disconcerted, sort of angry. I didn't understand. Finally he said, "Well maybe they didn't want him in Germany."

"You mean you didn't take him to London?"

"No! I took him to Berlin." He paused for a second, his eyes scanning the road ahead. "But, you know, it's cool, sometimes it happens like that. You have to go where the work is. Be prepared to travel if your boss asks you."

"Okay." I nodded eagerly. I would travel! I didn't mind moving around! I wanted him to know that I understood, that I was grown up and mature.

"There are jobs for waitresses in London," he said.

"Like serving food and stuff?"

"Yes. Exactly."

We sat in silence for a while and I thought about what it would be like to be a waitress in London. I imagined a busy, bustling restaurant full of stylish people, the loud chatter of intelligent conversation, food made from the best ingredients, me sweeping around the tables like a dancer, smiling and laughing and having the best time of my life. I read once in one of Tetya Svetlana's magazines about a new restaurant in Moscow. A place for the *Solntsevskaya*, the Mafia, who have all the money, but will also have you killed if you look at them the wrong way. The entrance was made of marble imported specially from Italy, and the food, they said, was the best in the world. The pictures showed beautiful waitresses in black dresses with clean white aprons.

"Will I have to wear a uniform?"

"Of course," he said. "You have to look good if you are going to work abroad. This is why we are going shopping." And he told me about the wonderful life in the West that was waiting for me. The life that is exactly the same as you read about in all the newspapers and magazines.

By the time we got into town it had started raining again so he parked the Land Rover right outside the row of stores where there was a McDonald's and a Zara and a Mexx and a cell phone shop and a branch of Pervomayskaya Zarya. He took me into Zara, where the clothes looked more expensive than I could ever afford. One small T-shirt cost the same as a week of Father's wages.

"Choose something you like," he said. "I've just got to make a phone call." He flipped open his cell phone and stepped outside.

I hid behind a row of winter coats and ran my hands through the soft wool and velvet. I didn't even know what size would fit me, and in the clean, bright space of the shop I could smell my dirty clothes and muddy boots. I felt the sales clerk staring at me, so I tried to look businesslike, as if I really belonged there in the clean world of new clothes and polished floorboards.

"Can I help you?"

The clerk towered over me, her lip curling up like a wet slug.

"Er . . ." I didn't know what to say. I pointed at Tommy, who was pacing up and down outside, gesticulating as he was talking. "I'm with him," I said.

"Ah." She raised an eyebrow. The kind of look that says *I know what you're doing*, except she didn't know anything at all.

"I'm going to London," I said. "To be a waitress."

"Ah," she said again. Then her eyes softened and she opened her mouth like she was about to ask me a question, but Tommy walked in and she backed off, busying herself folding sweaters into neat squares.

"What've you got?"

I picked out a red T-shirt and handed it to him. "Is that all?" I shrugged.

"You need more than that!" He looked around the store, flicking quickly through the aisles. I could feel the clerk staring but I didn't look over. He picked out some miniskirts, a blue blouse, a pair of jeans, and a thin top made out of floating see-through material. "Here. Try these on."

I went into the dressing room which, despite the modern-looking inside of the shop, was a dusty cupboard hidden by a thick cream curtain. There was an old dressing mirror propped up against the wall.

Everything was just a little too big. The miniskirts kept slipping down over my hips and the sleeves of the blouse fell over my hands. I could see my breasts through the floaty top. It was like I had shrunk inside the clothes, and my muddy boots made me look almost comical, like a clown.

When I went back into the shop, Tommy sighed. "Don't you have any smaller sizes?" he asked the clerk.

She stared at him. "We don't stock children's clothes in this store."

Tommy blinked. "I'll take them," he said, pulling out his wallet. "*All*." He counted out the notes slowly.

"Don't you want them wrapped?" she asked, staring at me as I tried to keep the skirt held up, hitching my thumb into the belt loop.

Then he said something really weird. He stopped counting out the money and leaned toward her and said, "I know people, you know."

She flicked her eyes away from him and started to add up the amount on her cash register.

Tommy turned to me and smiled, a wide, flashy grin.

"You need some shoes," he said, and wandered toward the side of the shop where there were shelves of shoes on the wall. "What size are you?"

He picked out a pair of blue sling backs with high heels and open toes and threw them on the floor in front of me.

"Try them on."

I kicked off my boots and stepped into the shoes. Instantly, I felt taller and more grown-up, although I couldn't walk. It was like standing on stilts or sharp stones. They were the kind of shoes Tetya Svetlana would put on the minute she got in from outside, taking off her fur-lined boots to change into something more elegant, high-heeled, usually with diamanté straps.

I wobbled but he didn't seem to notice. I wasn't sure I'd be able to waitress in such high shoes. I'd have to practice.

"We'll take them too."

The assistant wrapped up the clothes I wasn't wearing in fine sheets of tissue paper, like they were precious objects. I held on to my old clothes, not sure what to do with them. Tommy seemed impatient, tapping his foot and staring at the poster on the wall behind the cash register, a picture of a tall, beautiful woman, with pearly white teeth, modeling jeans and a crisp white shirt.

He snatched the bag away from the clerk when she was done.

Outside he seemed really angry and I wondered for a second if it was me, if I'd done anything wrong.

"Stupid bitch," he muttered as he leaned over the steering wheel to start the car.

After that, he took me to a hairdresser to get my hair cut, and then told me that he knew it was a personal matter, but girls my age needed good underwear, and he gave me some bills and made me go into Pervomayskaya Zarya and pick out some panties and a new bra.

When he mentioned underwear I got so ashamed I thought I might just burn up inside. I didn't want him to know that I never wore underwear. It wasn't that I didn't want to wear it, but in the choice between buying food for Viktor and new clothes, underwear lost out.

"Now, we need papers," Tommy said, when I got back in the car with my plastic bag full of panties.

"Papers?"

"*Passport*," he said in English, slowly, like I was dumb.

I didn't like the way that he was being impatient with me, and it was starting to get late in the afternoon. I was worried about Viktor. Kolya and Mikki would be bored of watching him by now. I just hoped they hadn't done anything stupid with him. "Can't we do that tomorrow?"

"No. Tonight. My friend is only in town tonight."

"Tonight? But I thought we were going back soon?"

"*No*." He stopped the car abruptly and turned to look at me.

155

"I *told* you. If you want a job, this is how it is. If you don't want to do it, that's up to you." He shrugged. "But then maybe you'd like to pay me for all those clothes? Eh? For wasting my time? If I thought you were going to be a baby about this I—"

"No! No!" I said. "It's okay." I tried to push the worry about Viktor to the back of my head. "I mean yes, I want to go." He had spent so much money on me, the thought of having to pay him back made me feel ill.

"Good."

He drove a few miles out of the city to the west, to a square of apartment blocks that were newer and cleaner than ours. On the balconies they had potted plants and furniture and awnings, and satellite dishes that stuck out of the walls like cartoon ears. There was even a new asphalt car park, although none of the cars parked in it were as new and flashy as the Land Rover.

"Come on."

It was already starting to get dark; the sun had dissolved into a line of light above the pine trees on the horizon. I shivered in my thin clothes, my legs came out in a rash of goosebumps and I stumbled in my heels. Tommy walked ahead of me like he was in a hurry. I trotted after him, holding my skirt up with my hand. Everything was suddenly moving too fast and I didn't like it.

"Is it the same as Adik?" I asked. "The same people who made the passport for him?"

"Yes," Tommy said.

That made me feel a bit safer. Adik was all right, so I was sure it would be the same for me. I couldn't imagine then what could possibly go wrong. I was going to London to get a job, that was it, simple. I didn't have any idea how I was going to get there, but it would be exciting. I was going to make money for Father and Viktor, and my mother would be proud of me, and Tommy was just a regular guy who wanted to give me a helping hand. I told myself that there wasn't anything to be afraid of, it was all going to be cool, and before I knew it I would see Adik and we would marvel together at our lucky escape and our new lives, just like we always dreamed we would.

It makes me want to laugh now, when I think how stupid I was, like a deer in winter, driven from the trees by the frozen ground in which nothing can grow. Slowly sniffing its way out of safety, knowing that going back means it will probably die from hunger, and that if it goes forward it will have to run faster than the men with shotguns who lurk around the edges of the forest. The weather makes it easy for the hunters, they don't even have to track it. Just lay a trail of food, and hang around, sipping on their flasks of vodka, waiting for the prey to come to them.

19

Oksana

Inside the apartment was a warm, steamy aura of cooking and cigarettes. The minute I got inside I wondered why I'd been so nervous. There was a woman in the kitchen at the stove, stirring a boiling pan of pasta, and the man who opened the door to us grinned and shook my hand like I was an old member of his family.

"Welcome, welcome." He was almost bowing as I walked behind Tommy into the living room where there was a huge sofa, a big TV, a computer, a desk and stacks of winking electronic equipment.

"Sit down! Be comfortable!"

There was another girl there too, who I knew from the village as Katya. She didn't look up from the war film that was on the TV, just grunted as I sank down on the sofa next to her.

"Is this her?" the man asked, pointing at me. He was a thin, wiry guy with a cigarette tucked behind his ear. He had a gold front tooth instead of a real one, which made him look like a pirate when he smiled.

"Yes," Tommy said.

"Okay." He pursed his lips and looked at me. "Could you stand up again, sweetheart, just for a second. I need to measure your height."

I stood up again and he leaned back from me and pinched his chin, like he was trying to figure out something.

"Sixteen with a bit of makeup," he said, shaking his head and smiling at me. "It's a reach. You really know how to pick them, Tom boy."

Tommy grinned and lit a cigarette. He flopped onto the sofa next to the girl, who was still staring glassy-eyed at the screen: men running and yelling and lots of shouting, shooting and explosions. It was so loud it was kind of distracting.

"Okay, out here, if you don't mind."

I followed the man down the corridor into another room. Here there was a camera and a tripod and a sleek laptop set up on a desk next to a big double bed.

"You got any makeup, sweetheart?"

"No."

He sucked his teeth and said, "Tommy, Tommy, Tommy." Then he shouted. "Hey, Katya! Can I borrow some of your makeup?"

There was no reply.

"Go into the bathroom, sweetheart, put on some makeup. You know, a little lipstick." He drew an imaginary line across his lips.

On the way back down the corridor to the bathroom, I passed the kitchen again. The woman was still in there, pouring water into a kettle. She looked up and smiled at me. Her face was doughy and sweaty, bright red hair tucked behind her ears.

"Hey!" She beckoned me into the kitchen. "Welcome!" She kissed me on both cheeks. "Call me Mama! You look like you need some hot food. Tonight! You will eat with us!"

"Oh," I said, "I'm sorry, I have to go home." Tempting as the food smells were, it was getting dangerously late, and even if Tommy drove really fast I wasn't sure we would get home before Father got back from work.

She frowned. "Home? They said you were here for the work."

159

"Oh yes! I am!"

"Then you stay for dinner. I would take it personally if you didn't."

Suddenly there seemed to be so many rules; it made me confused. "But I have to go home, to my brother. I have to watch him."

"Your brother? Didn't Tommy take care of that?"

"No, he only paid Kolya and Mikki to watch him for the afternoon!"

But it was like she wasn't listening. "You know, you worry too much, and worry, it makes people grow old before their time. You are young, you need to live a little. Here you are in my apartment, ready to leave on an adventure and already you want to go home!"

"No, I didn't mean that!"

"Of course you didn't!" She smiled and touched my face and in spite of the heat in the kitchen her hands were icy cold. "Go and get ready for Pitor, sweetheart. I know he wants his dinner too."

In the small bathroom there were two makeup cases on top of the toilet cistern. I found some pink lipstick and mascara and, as I applied them, I wondered what the woman had meant about me being ready to leave on an adventure. I wasn't ready to go anywhere yet. I had to say good-bye to Father, organize someone to take care of Viktor. They were moving too fast. I didn't remember telling Tommy I was ready to go away right now, but then I wasn't sure if he'd said something and maybe I wasn't listening closely.

I told myself that maybe they needed waitresses right now and that was why everyone was in such a hurry. And anyway, it was a luxurious apartment and Pitor and Call-Me-Mama seemed kind and helpful. I was being paranoid, I told myself as I brushed mascara over my eyelashes. This was the start of my new life and I was spoiling the moment by getting scared.

It took about ten minutes for Pitor to take my photo. He had to set up the lighting just right, he said. He told me to sit on the chair in the middle of the room, while he fussed around with a white sheet and a lamp. When he was done, my picture came up on the screen. I could see that the way he had taken it was so the shadows fell across my face, emphasizing my cheekbones, making me look older.

"And now you are Miss Leola Maldini." He fetched a piece of paper from his printer. On it was a page of a passport with my face on it, but it didn't have my name on it and in the details of birth it said I was *Italian*.

"I thought I was going to work in England?"

Pitor didn't answer immediately. He fiddled with his computer and changed the color of my face from pale to tanned. He moved the mouse and rubbed away the dark lines under my eyes, and made my lips sparkle and turned my eyes a bright white.

"England, Italy, Germany—with this you can work anywhere you like in Europe."

He printed the picture out again. Now I looked like a model, like a clean, healthy, improved version of myself.

"Beautiful, huh?" He leaned over my shoulder so I could feel his breath on my cheek. "A girl can go far," he said, "with a face like that."

After that we had dinner, although we didn't really eat together, like they said. Tommy and Pitor sat together with the laptop computer, working while they ate. I sat next to Katya on the sofa and ate in silence, staring at the TV.

I couldn't eat much. I just stirred the pasta around with my

161

fork, tried to make it look smaller on the plate by piling it high. My stomach started to hurt after only a few mouthfuls, even though it tasted like heaven, because I was still trying to figure out a way to ask Tommy when we could go home, and when we did, how I would explain everything to Father.

Time seemed to drag on until eventually I stood up and said brightly, "Well, thank you very much for dinner, but really I've got to go home now."

Tommy and Pitor looked over at me and stared, then they both burst out laughing.

"Hey, girl! Relax!" Pitor said. "Here, have some vodka!" He poured a shot into a plastic cup and handed it to me. "Drink!" he said. "To your new job!"

I lifted it to my lips and drank. The alcohol burned as it touched my lips, making me wince. I only liked vodka when it was cold and I was outside with Adik and our guts were on fire and we were laughing about stupid things and making ourselves woozy by running around and around in the snow, like fireworks gone off in the wrong direction.

"Sit down! Sit down!" Tommy waved his hand at me. "We're not going anywhere now!"

"You will stay the night!" Pitor said.

"But I have to go home! My brother—"

"SIT DOWN!" Tommy yelled, making my heart jump. He got up and leaped across the room and stood in front of me. A muscle twitched in his cheek. "Stop moaning!"

"But—"

"NOW!"

I thought he was going to hit me. Tears sprang into my eyes. Then Call-Me-Mama came bustling in between us. "Hey, hey," and she muttered something to Tommy which could have been "not yet" or "not now."

I sat back shakily on the sofa next to Katya. I wondered if

she ever did anything except stare at the TV. She was still staring, even though Tommy was standing right in the way of the screen.

"Look, sweetheart," Call-Me-Mama said, her face getting serious. "You want to get a job and go to work in England? You're going to have to stay cool, like Katya here, okay?"

Stay cool? Every second I was in that apartment was starting to feel like a horrible mistake. I looked at Katya, who acknowledged me by grunting.

"Is it true? Are you going too?"

She bit her thumbnail and nodded.

"Tonight you are staying here and tomorrow you go to Poland, and then to London. Just like Tommy explained," Call-Me-Mama said. "So everybody just needs to stay *cool*."

I pressed my lips together and stared at the TV screen behind Tommy's legs. Then I told myself I was being unfair and that it was kind of these people to help me out and organize everything for me. I was behaving like a kid, like Viktor when he wanted something he couldn't have. I had to calm down and grow up. Viktor would be all right—Kolya would get bored of playing with him eventually and they'd take him back to Father. And I was going on an adventure; I was going to earn money and have a life. I could call and tell Father everything when I got there. I just kept focusing on the thought of me, with a platter held high above my head, weaving and twisting between tables of rich and beautiful diners like I was dancing; the best waitress in the whole world.

Katya and I slept in the same room on sagging bunk beds. Call-Me-Mama even gave us some towels and kissed us on both cheeks and told us we were lucky to be getting out of the country and how she wished she was young enough to come with us too. After she closed the door, I heard the soft click of a bolt sliding into place.

Katya didn't seem to notice so I didn't say anything. Maybe it was just a safety precaution, I told myself. People like Pitor and Call-Me-Mama had a lot of stuff. Perhaps they were afraid of burglars.

Katya turned her back to me and got undressed. She put on a thin nylon nightgown with bright cartoon teddy bears on it. Now that we were alone together, there were so many questions I wanted to ask her.

"Where is your family?"

She shrugged. "Nowhere."

"Are you coming with me? To be a waitress?"

"Yeah, right," she snorted.

"To London?" I folded my new clothes into a neat pile on the dresser. I pulled out my dirty old T-shirt and put it on to sleep in, self-conscious about the fact that it was torn and nearly worn to pieces. I would buy myself some new T-shirts when I got my first wages.

"Top bunk is mine," Katya said, climbing up, the springs creaking as she shifted around making herself comfortable. "Turn off the light before you lie down." And she turned over to face the wall.

I lay under the thin covers, listening to her breathing. It didn't sound like she could sleep either—she kept turning over and sighing really heavily.

I must have fallen asleep because for a second I didn't know where I was. The room was so dark and there was no Viktor cuddling close to me under the blankets like a cat.

"*Shhhh.*" The hand pushed down on my mouth so hard I thought my neck was going to snap. I was too shocked to scream. All I could hear was heavy breathing and the squeak of the bedsprings as he lay on top of me. It was Pitor. His beard was scratchy against my cheek and he smelled of vodka and cigarettes. He whispered names in my ear, dirty names— *whore, bitch, telka*. I tried to struggle, but I couldn't move. I wondered if Katya could hear, and why she didn't make a noise, or start protesting. Between the two of us we could have fought him off.

Then he said in a loud whisper: "If you scream I will kill you and then I will kill your family." And then it really hurt and I bit his hand, hard, but he just kept pressing down until I thought I would pass out and in my head I shouted out for my mother and Viktor and my father, and in that second, suddenly, I understood everything.

When he was gone, I lay in the bed too sore and shocked to move. I wanted to find Tommy and tell him that it wasn't safe here, to take me home, now. But I knew the door was locked and I was too frightened to make a noise in case Pitor came back. Then I started to feel very bad about Viktor and Father and I thought that it had only happened as a punishment against me. Because I was a bad and neglectful daughter who bad-mouthed her dead mother and wouldn't do what her father told her and didn't take care of her brother like she was supposed to.

"Stop crying."

Katya's voice surprised me. She sounded wide awake. The bed grated as she turned over again. "Don't think about it," she mumbled into the mattress.

But I couldn't not think about it. When Call-Me-Mama came in a few hours later and got us out of bed, I wanted to tell her, but every time I tried to make the sentences in my head, I couldn't get a hold of the right words. Besides, I was ashamed. Ashamed that Katya had heard it, ashamed as if, by my stupidity, I had *made* him do it to me.

"The car is ready now," Call-Me-Mamma said, giving us plastic bags with a few apples and a bottle of Coke. "Come on." She prodded me in the back when I tried to dawdle in the doorway.

When we got outside, Pitor was behind the wheel of a Volkswagen, the engine running, fumes from the exhaust making clouds in the cold, early-morning air. There was no sign of Tommy, or of Tommy's Land Rover.

"Hey, sweetheart," Pitor said, winking at me. He waved his hand, showing my teeth marks on his palm. "Get in."

"Where's Tommy?"

"He had business to attend to. I'm taking you over the border."

I couldn't look at him, his smile made me feel sick. Over the border, farther away from home than I had ever been in my life.

"Um, it's okay," I said. "I think I've changed—" But Call-Me-Mama was behind me. She grabbed me around the waist and pushed me toward the car.

"Get in," she growled. "Don't be a troublemaker. Or you'll get a reputation. And then you won't get any work."

Pitor opened the passenger door. "You can sit next to me," he smirked.

Pitor drove fast, with the heating on high so the air in the car was dry and stuffy. Katya fell asleep, lolling on the backseat, waking up every time Pitor took a sharp turn, because her skull would slap against the window.

She whined at him to slow down but he ignored her. Driving south, relentlessly, mile after mile along the bad, bumpy road. We hit a bunch of rainstorms, one after the other, the clouds bubbling up on the horizon thick and black, like smoke. As we drove through them rain came down in heavy sheets, as if some great babushka was rinsing out her backyard, slopping pails of water straight at us.

As the day wore on into evening, we joined a main road, where huge trucks thundered all around us, wheels throwing up spray and dirt. We passed forests and meadows and fields, and as the sun went down all I could see were the taillights of the trucks, little glowing coals that showed us the way ahead.

We got to the border about midnight. Just before we got there, Pitor pulled over. He opened the glove compartment of the car and pulled out three passports, and then something which made my stomach clench: a gun.

"See that?" he said, nodding at his lap. "If you try anything I will shoot you. Understand?"

I nodded.

He laid the passports open on the dashboard and counted out some money, slipping a wad of notes into each one.

"Just a little lubrication," he said, his gold tooth glinting.

As we got closer I could see a series of low huts clustered around a pair of red and white barriers. Men in military uniform were talking to the drivers, peering in through the windows of the cars with flashlights. The whole place was lit up with dazzling lights like the kind they have at night-time soccer games on TV.

"If you say anything, either of you, I will shoot you."

Katya snorted. "It's okay," she said. "It's not like I haven't done this before."

The guard had his collar turned up over his cheeks. He didn't even say hello as he took the passports that Pitor handed to him out of the window. When they were returned the wads of money were gone.

"Move along now, please," he said, waving us forward.

167

"Ha!" Pitor laughed softly to himself. "The miracle of money! Did you see that? Did you see how money *talks*?"

Money talks. I thought about that for a long time afterward. All the way through the Ukraine and then into Moldova, at every checkpoint, always the same routine. I wondered what money would really say if I could hear it talking. Would it tell the truth, or would it tell lies? Would it tell me what was going to happen to me when we got to our destination? Would it scream for help when we stopped for gas in Romania? What would it say about all the greasy hands it had passed through on its way to the cash registers of stores or the counters at the bank?

When I fell asleep, I dreamed of notes floating around my head, swirling like leaves in a storm, but every time I tried, I couldn't catch one, even though they were flying past my face. And all the time I could hear the money chattering in my head; every single note talking all at once so I couldn't make out the words. But as I listened the sound started to change and become like a rhythm and the rhythm became the constant pounding of an engine, drumming out a single word, *more . . . more . . . more . . . more . . . more . . .* So loud I thought it would make me deaf.

20

Hope

He told me to wait. So I am standing with my ear pressed to the door, listening. It's evening now. The light around the drywall has faded to a pink glow from the sodium lights outside. I can hear the front door slamming downstairs—it makes the building shake every time it shuts, a heavy crash—and voices talking.

When Oksana comes back from her shift I will tell her and we'll go together. The idea of leaving her here makes me feel sick and I'm not sure I can make it on my own anyway. I don't know what to do about the Estonians, they're too stoned to run away. They'll be a liability. Perhaps it would be better to have the police come back and get them. I pace the room; Oksana will know what to do.

Then the front door slams again and there are voices talking, Fat Burger Man laughing and spitting. One voice gets closer, a shout at the bottom of the stairs, then footsteps coming closer.

The floorboards outside creak, there's a key in the lock, then Latif is in the room.

He stares at me for a second and I can feel all the blood drain out of my face. My skin turns cold and gray and I'm sure he can see the shape of keys in my pocket.

"It is a shame you will soon be going. I think my little cousin

169

likes you," he says eventually. Then he laughs and shakes his head, and passes me a Burger King bag. "For you."

He slams the door shut and locks it. I don't dare move. Latif's heavy feet on the stairs make the mattress vibrate. I want to unlock the door right now and take my chances. See if I can't sneak between their legs and grab Oksana and together we can slip out too quickly for them to catch us. It takes all my concentration to force myself to sit still. Fazil said to wait until later. I know that I've only got one chance and I can't blow it.

Oksana comes back with Lulu and Ekaterina about midnight. The minute Latif and Babalan have locked us in again the Estonians fumble in their bags for their drug stuff. Ekaterina silently unfolds a square of foil, pressing it flat against her thigh.

Oksana lies on the bed next to me. Her face is weary and there is a dark bruise spreading on her stomach from this morning. I wonder why men think she is sexy; she is dirty and skinny and tired, not glossy and shiny like in the videos and magazines.

I glance over at the Estonians but they can't see anything except their drugs.

"Look," I whisper proudly, pulling one of the keys out of my pocket so she can see. Oksana stares. "For the door."

For a moment her pupils grow huge. Then she flops down onto the bed and turns her head away from me. "Good luck then."

"Aren't you coming with me?!" I sit on the bed, shake her by the shoulder. "You *can't* stay here."

She shrugs. "What is the point? What is the point of Natasha trying to get out of here? Natasha can't escape. This is all she deserves." And she sweeps her arm around the room.

"Don't say that!" My voice rises. "It's not your *fault*."

170

It's not hers and it's not mine.

Lulu looks over at us. "Stop bitching," she says. Except she pronounces it like "beeching."

"We're not bitching." I say. "We're—"

"Talking about asking them if we can take a bath," Oksana cuts in, pointing at the door.

Lulu shrugs and turns back to the thin line of powder in the foil.

"Don't tell them," Oksana hisses at me. "Don't trust them. They are in with the Turkish; they get drugs here." She lies back on the bed and stares at the ceiling. "Wait for them to go to sleep." Then she turns away from me again.

I go back to my bed and watch her back, rising and falling as she breathes. No one in their right mind would choose to be here. I'm not leaving her behind, I'll carry her if I have to.

Eventually, Lulu and Ekaterina climb under the sheets and appear to go to sleep. Lulu sleeps with her mouth open, a white ball of spit collecting in the corner. I get up and turn off the lights. The darkness covers us like a thick blanket. It takes a while for my eyes to get adjusted but there is enough street-lamp light seeping round the drywall edges for me to be able to make out the shape of the beds, the whites of Oksana's eyes, glinting. She is facing me now.

"Oksana, *please*," I whisper. "You *have* to come with me. I can't do this on my own."

"I have no papers. They arrest me, send me home. You go," she hisses.

I reach across the gap between our beds and grab her hand. "I won't tell the police about you. I *promise*."

"No!" Her voice gets louder. "No police!"

My heart skips. We can't have this conversation now. "No. It's okay. *Shhhhh*."

In desperation I try one last time. "Oksana, come with me."

I make her look at me. "Leave Natasha here and come with me. *Please.*"

"You don't know me!" she says sharply.

And for a second I think she's going to fight me. But then she squeezes my hand back and sighs. "Will you help me to find Tottenham?" she says more gently.

"Yes."

She sighs again and stands up. "Okay."

I almost laugh out loud with relief. But instead, I get up and tiptoe over to the door. I press my ear against the wood and try to listen. I can't hear anything. I wonder if there's anyone sitting outside. Fazil told me to watch out for the CCTV, but I can't remember where he said it was. Stupid. My mind races and I gasp for breath like a swimmer surfacing. I have to remind myself to *breathe.*

"Oksana?" I whisper.

"Yes."

"Let's go."

I pull the keys out of my pocket, fumbling a little as I try the wrong key first. My fingers don't seem to want to be quick. I take another deep breath. This time the right key. It fits the lock and the barrel turns with a soft click. Carefully, I push the handle down and gingerly pull the door open, inch by inch until I can just put my head in the gap and peek out. The corridor is dark, lit only from downstairs by the dingy electric light that shines up the stairwell at the far end. There's a gray plastic chair next to our door like the ones at school, where I guess the person who's supposed to guard us sits.

I hold another breath, wait, in case someone heard, then we step out into the semidarkness of the corridor. I shut the door behind us, but I don't lock the Estonians in, just in case.

Oksana presses herself against the wall and tiptoes to the top of the stairs. We both stand and listen. There's the smell of a fresh cigarette and the sound of a radio, maybe a TV, coming from one of the rooms.

"Security, he's still awake," Oksana says in my ear. "We have to wait."

We sit side by side on the top stair, the thick, greasy green carpet makes me itchy just to look at it. There's a cough and a grunt and I can feel Oksana's arms tensing. I stand up, but I don't know if I should run back to the room or stay where I am. Then, nothing. We listen for a bit longer.

Now, I think. We should be going now. But I can't move.

"Come on." Oksana grabs my hand and pulls me up. "We go."

Very, very slowly we go down the stairs, one by one. Me first, holding my breath until the blood in my head gets too noisy. I can see the bolted door and the iron gate with the padlock on it. Along the corridor on the middle floor, there's a door ajar on the left, and the drone of a soccer commentator and the roars and chants of a crowd.

"He's in the kitchen," Oksana hisses. "He can't see."

We run down the rest of the stairs on tiptoes to reach the gate. The front door is just an arm's stretch away. My hands are clammy as I try to get the right key into the gate padlock— it fits, but it won't turn.

"I can't do it!" I wiggle the key in the lock. There's another grunt from the kitchen, louder and closer this time.

"Quick!" Oksana grabs the key. "Let me try."

The gate rattles as she pulls the padlock toward her. "It's not working!" she hisses.

The frustration makes my throat itch and my eyes water. We're so close. I pull the gate toward me and it clanks loudly on its hinges. We stand still, frozen like deer in headlights. The soccer commentary goes off with a snap and there's a sniff and the scrape of a chair being pulled back.

173

Oksana's still fiddling with the keys. "Come on, come on," she says. And then the lock springs, just in time.

"*What?!*" He stands above us at the top of the first flight of stairs, staring at us blearily. "What?"

"Quick!" Oksana grabs my hand as she flips open all the bolts and locks on the front door, clanging the metal gate shut behind us.

In a second we are out on the sidewalk.

"*Run!*"

My legs feel light and rubbery. There's no time to think.

"Hey!" he roars after us.

I don't look even though I know he's right behind us, fumbling with his car keys.

"Over here!" I cross the road and turn down a side street, into an alleyway round the back of some houses, cats jump out of our way, or eye us warily from behind the Dumpsters. We just can't get caught. Not again. We run and run.

But then, at the end of an alley, is a wall, topped with broken glass and bits of wire. Shit. We're blocked in. We drop down quickly behind a Dumpster.

"Did he see us?"

"I don't know."

Then there's the crunch of footsteps and I can see the shape of a man peering down the alleyway toward us.

"It's him!" Oksana slumps next to me. "What are we going to do?"

I won't give up. There is a way out of this. "Up there!" We have to go over the wall. I jump up on the Dumpster and balance, like a tightrope walker, arms out to steady myself. "Quick!"

I grab Oksana's hand and pull her up behind me.

The man has seen us now and he shouts and starts lumbering faster toward us. I don't have time to be scared. It's just like climbing the trees at home I tell myself. Branch to branch, higher and higher like a cat.

It's over in a second. One of those moves that if you showed me how to do it I would panic and say no way. But I have a picture in my head of what my body has to do and while I'm thinking about leaping over the wall without cutting my feet to shreds, I'm suddenly there with Oksana holding my hand and together we're leaping off an almost ten feet high wall into the unknown of someone's back garden.

"Oomph."

"Ow!"

We land on a compost heap, silted up against the wall. It stinks of onions and garlic and slimy garbage. We're over.

"Are you okay?"

"Yes."

We stand up, getting our bearings. My shoes are covered in muck and I've ripped my trousers, all the way down from the knee. Underneath I can see I've cut myself; there's a thin trickle of blood on my leg. But now my eyes have adjusted it's clear we're in one of a whole row of back gardens. Somehow we need to find a way out of here too.

A face appears on top of the wall and Oksana pulls me back into the undergrowth. He's too fat and chicken to jump over. He's breathing like a horse, harrumphing and wheezing.

"Over here." Oksana creeps along next to the wall, crunching leaves and undergrowth. He can probably hear us, but he can't see us. The fence between the houses is broken at the bottom of the garden and we just have to step through it to reach the garden of the house next door.

The security light dazzles us. Lights flicker on inside the house.

"Shit!"

We crouch down behind a clump of tall irises. We look at

each other. "I have to go," Oksana says. "You stay here, to call police."

There's a woman's face at the downstairs window peering out. Then the back door opens.

"Hey!" A man in a bathrobe, holding a flashlight, stands on his patio, squinting into the garden. "My wife's calling the police, you know!"

"It's okay. You trust him," Oksana says.

"How do you know?"

She points at the red climbing frame and the blue paddling pool. "They have children."

"I don't want to leave you," I say. "Will you be okay?"

She sucks her teeth. "I will be okay, a cat with many lives. Now go! You talk, I find Tottenham." Then she smiles at me. "*Hope.* You were lucky when your mother gave you your name. She will be so happy to know you are free. And you have been a good friend. Natasha is sorry she got you into trouble."

I don't know what to say as I hug her good-bye. "Will you let me know that you're okay somehow?"

She flutters her hands in front of her face, maybe to hide the fact that there are tears spilling down her cheeks. "Yes, yes, now you go. Go! Go on!" The man in the bathrobe is starting to walk toward us. "Quick!"

Slowly, with my hands up, I walk out of the flower bed on to the lawn.

"Help me," I say, my knees trembling. "My name is Hope Tasker and I need to talk to the police."

As I walk toward him, I'm aware of Oksana scuttling back into the undergrowth next door, darting and weaving out of sight. When I turn to check, she's vanished into the shadows like she was never there.

*

The policewoman who interviews me is very nice. She brings me a cup of hot cocoa and a chocolate bar.

"Only out of the machine, I'm afraid," she says, putting a reassuring hand on my shoulder.

Mum and Dad are driving down the highway right now. I spoke to them on Mr. Patterson's phone. Mum was too emotional to say much—she kept swallowing her words and crying. Even though I told her that, really, I was fine.

"Just stay there," Dad said. "We're coming to get you. Don't move." The line crackled. "I love you."

Mr. Patterson said he was shocked that there was a brothel above the fish and chips shop in the next street.

"The sign says Sauna," he said.

The police send some squad cars over to search the place, but when they get there it's empty, although there's "evidence that the premises were vacated in a hurry."

"Don't worry," the policewoman says, shuffling her papers in front of her. "We'll catch them."

I'm feeling strangely calm, almost detached. I study the scruffy paintwork of the police station. It smells a bit like a hospital.

"So," she says, "in your own time. Tell me exactly what happened."

I take a sip of the hot, sweet chocolate and wonder where I should begin.

21

Oksana

Now there's a big road and a junction and traffic lights and cars. My feet are sore from running so hard and my legs are covered in scratches and cuts. On the road signs it said it was this way to Tottenham. But now I'm here, and I don't know which road to take. I don't know how I will find Adik. Perhaps I expected some big flashing arrow pointing the way. All I had to do was get to Tottenham and I would immediately bump into him, or his house would appear all lit up, so I would know where to find him.

I need to ask where Lordship Road is but I don't want anyone to notice me. What if they report me to the police? And I have to fight with myself not to just sit down on the sidewalk and wait for someone to carry me. I'm so tired. Tired of running, of hiding, of being scared, and dirty.

It's almost day. The sky is starting to turn gray, and there are more people walking along, their heads bent low, hands in their pockets. No one even looks at me.

I stand at a bus stop and stare at the map, but it doesn't make any sense. There are numbers for all the buses that will take you places, but I don't know where anything is: Finsbury Park, Aldgate, Alexandra Palace—maybe I should go there and visit with the Queen. That thought makes me dizzy. That if I wanted I could go and see the Queen, that I could learn the streets all for myself. That I could be free.

Buses come and go and I sit there like I'm waiting for something to happen. The crowds get bigger with people jostling to get to work. So many people, speaking all different languages. I actually hear some girls talking Russian and hide behind an advertisement for shaving cream till they get on their bus to Bethnal Green.

"Are you all right, love?"

The woman has a kindly face, soft and floury. I stare at her for a second, then show her the scrap of postcard in my hand and point at the address.

"You want Lordship Road?"

I nod.

"It's just over there, second on your left."

She points across the road from where I've been sitting, which makes me smile. All the time it was right in front of me—a miracle.

"Thank you," I whisper.

"That's okay." She cocks her head to one side, like she's trying to see deeper inside me. She reminds me a bit of Mum. "Look after yourself," she says, turning away.

Maybe Mum is up there still, looking out for me, and today she is singing because she knows I am set free too. My heart takes a little leap. Here I am at last, Adik, after all this time.

The road is a row of houses all stuck together, like a lot of the houses around here. They make me think of people standing in a line, pressing together shoulder to shoulder, jostling each other for space. It's hard to imagine him living here. The road seems so quiet and rich. The numbers count down from 260, so it's a long way farther down the road. I wonder as I get closer what his room will look like, what he's doing here for money. It has occurred to me that he might still be working for Tommy, but if Tommy is there, I tell myself, I *will* run to the police, even though I don't think my legs will carry me much farther. Besides, I remember how Tommy looked that time I told him Adik was in London, not Germany. I didn't know it then, but Tommy was surprised, and not that happy either. I hope that means Adik got away.

Number eighty-eight. The door is red and freshly painted, and there's a miniature tree in a pot right outside the front window, cut into a kind of corkscrew shape.

It looks like a rich house, like he is doing well for himself. My chest is proud for him, he must have made it, I think. Like he always said he would.

I knock on the door and a dog barks somewhere inside. I bite my lip. What if it's not him?

The door opens carefully and I can see a dog's nose sniffing the air, and then a man with silvery gray hair appears in the corridor.

"Hello?" He looks at me curiously. "Are you okay?"

I am frozen to the doormat. I've made a terrible mistake. Of course Adik isn't here, in a place like this. Suddenly I want to lie down and cry, right there on the doorstep in front of the old man who takes another step toward me. I take a few steps back toward the gate. The old man doesn't look like he will hurt me, but I have learned that you can never tell. "Hey, are you all right?"

"Adik?" I manage hopelessly.

"Oh!" The man's eyes widen as if suddenly he understands something, then he smiles gently at me. "I should have guessed. Just stay there a minute. He's in the garden. I'll go and get him."

Adik *is* here. The dog comes out and sniffs around my legs. I stroke him on the head and marvel at how warm and safe he feels. I wonder if this man helped Adik to get away.

And then Adik is there in front of me, face paling with shock, and we're just staring at each other. Trying to figure out how come we both look so different, so much *older*, than we did before.

"Oksana!" He lets the door close behind him and grabs me in a huge bear hug. "What happened to you? What the hell are you doing here?"

I look at him and take a deep breath, and try to think of where I should begin.